Dec. 2nd 2000

Dear Reader,

Looking back over the years, I find it hard to realise that twenty-six of them have gone by since I wrote my first book—*Sister Peters in Amsterdam*. It wasn't until I started writing about her that I found that once I had started writing, nothing was going to make me stop—and at that time I had no intention of sending it to a publisher. It was my daughter who urged me to try my luck.

I shall never forget the thrill of having my first book accepted. A thrill I still get each time a new story is accepted. Writing to me is such a pleasure, and seeing a story unfolding on my old typewriter is like watching a film and wondering how it will end. Happily of course.

To have so many of my books re-published is such a delightful thing to happen and I can only hope that those who read them will share my pleasure in seeing them on the bookshelves again...and enjoy reading them.

D0892152

Back by Popular Demand

A collector's edition of favourite titles from one of the world's best-loved romance authors. Mills & Boon® are proud to bring back these sought after titles and present them as one cherished collection.

BETTY NEELS: COLLECTOR'S EDITION

NANNY BY CHANCE

BY
BETTY NEELS

MILLS & BOON®

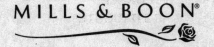

*First published in Great Britain 1998 by Mills & Boon Limited,
This edition 2000
Harlequin Mills & Boon Limited,
Eton House, 18-24 Paradise Road, Richmond, Surrey TW9 1SR*

© Betty Neels 1998

ISBN 0 263 82466 7

73-0401

*Printed and bound in Spain
by Litografia Rosés S.A., Barcelona*

CHAPTER ONE

ARAMINTA POMFREY, a basket of groceries over one arm, walked unhurriedly along the brick path to the back door, humming as she went. She was, after all, on holiday, and the morning was fine, the autumn haze slowly lifting to promise a pleasant September day—the first of the days ahead of doing nothing much until she took up her new job.

She paused at the door to scratch the head of the elderly, rather battered cat sitting there. An old warrior if ever there was one, with the inappropriate name of Cherub. He went in with her, following her down the short passage and into the kitchen, where she put her basket on the table, offered him milk and then, still humming, went across the narrow hall to the sitting room.

Her mother and father would be there, waiting for her to return from the village shop so that they might have coffee together. The only child of elderly parents, she had known from an early age that although they loved her dearly, her unexpected late arrival had upset their established way of life. They were clever, both authorities on ancient Celtic history, and had published books on the subject—triumphs of knowledge even if they didn't do much to boost their finances.

Not that either of them cared about that. Her father had a small private income, which allowed them to live precariously in the small house his father had left him, and they had sent Araminta to a good school, confident that she would follow in their footsteps and become a literary genius of some sort. She had done her best, but the handful of qualifications she had managed to get had been a disappointment to them, so that when she had told them that she would like to take up some form of nursing, they had agreed with relief.

There had been no question of her leaving home and training at some big hospital; her parents, their heads in Celtic clouds, had no time for household chores or cooking. The elderly woman who had coped while Araminta was at school had been given her notice and Araminta took over the housekeeping while going each day to a children's convalescent home at the other end of the village. It hadn't been quite what she had hoped for, but it had been a start.

And now, five years later, fate had smiled kindly upon her. An elderly cousin, recently widowed, was coming to run the house for her mother and father and Araminta was free to start a proper training. And about time too, she had reflected, though probably she would be considered too old to start training at twenty-three. But her luck had held; in two weeks' time she was to start as a student nurse at a London teaching hospital.

Someone was with her parents. She opened the door and took a look. Dr Jenkell, a family friend as well as their doctor for many years.

She bade him good morning and added, 'I'll fetch the coffee.' She smiled at her mother and went back to the kitchen, to return presently with a tray laden with cups and saucers, the coffeepot and a plate of biscuits.

'Dr Jenkell has some splendid news for you, Araminta,' said her mother. 'Not too much milk, dear.' She took the cup Araminta offered her and sat back, looking pleased about something.

Araminta handed out coffee and biscuits. She said, 'Oh?' in a polite voice, drank some coffee and then, since the doctor was looking at her, added, 'Is it something very exciting?'

Dr Jenkell wiped some coffee from his drooping moustache. 'I have a job for you, my dear. A splendid opportunity. Two small boys who are to go and live for a short time with their uncle in Holland while their parents are abroad. You have had a good deal of experience dealing with the young and I hear glowing accounts of you at the children's home. I was able to recommend you with complete sincerity.'

Araminta drew a steadying breath. 'I've been taken as a student nurse at St Jules'. I start in two weeks' time.' She added, 'I told you and you gave me a reference.'

Dr Jenkell waved a dismissive hand. 'That's easily arranged. All you need to do is to write and say that you are unable to start training for the time being. A month or so makes no difference.'

'It does to me,' said Araminta. 'I'm twenty-three, and if I don't start my training now I'll be too old.' She refilled his coffee cup with a steady hand. 'It's very kind of you, and I do appreciate it, but it means a lot to me—training for something I really want to do.'

She glanced at her mother and father and the euphoria of the morning ebbed way; they so obviously sided with Dr Jenkell.

'Of course you must take this post Dr Jenkell has so kindly arranged for you,' said her mother. 'Indeed, you cannot refuse, for I understand that he has already promised that you will do so. As for your training, a few months here or there will make no difference at all. You have all your life before you.'

'You accepted this job for me without telling me?' asked Araminta of the doctor.

Her father spoke then. 'You were not here when the offer was made. Your mother and I agreed that it was a splendid opportunity for you to see something of the world and agreed on your behalf. We acted in your best interests, my dear.'

I'm a grown woman, thought Araminta wildly, and I'm being treated like a child, a mid-Victorian child at that, meekly accepting what her elders and betters have decided was best for her. Well, I won't, she reflected, looking at the three elderly faces in turn.

'I think that, if you don't mind, Dr Jenkell, I'll go and see this uncle.'

Dr Jenkell beamed at her. 'That's right, my dear— get some idea of what is expected of you. You'll find him very sympathetic to any adjustments you may have in mind.'

Araminta thought this unlikely, but she wasn't going to say so. She loved her parents and they loved her, although she suspected that they had never quite got over the surprise of her arrival in their early middle age. She wasn't going to upset them now; she would see this man, explain why she couldn't accept the job and then think of some way of telling her parents which wouldn't worry them. Dr Jenkell might be annoyed; she would think about that later.

Presently the doctor left and she collected the coffee cups and went along to the kitchen to unpack her shopping and prepare the lunch, leaving her mother and father deep in a discussion of the book of Celtic history they were writing together. They hadn't exactly forgotten her. The small matter of her future having been comfortably settled, they felt free to return to their abiding interest…

As she prepared the lunch, Araminta laid her plans. Dr Jenkell had given her the uncle's address, and unless he'd seen fit to tell the man that she intended visiting him she would take him by surprise, explain that she wasn't free to take the job and that would be that. There was nothing like striking while the iron was hot. It would be an easy enough journey; Hambledon was barely three miles from Henley-on-Thames and she could be in London in no time at all. She would go the very next day…

Her mother, apprised of her intention, made no objection. Indeed, she was approving. 'As long as you leave something ready for our lunch, Araminta. You know how impatient your father is if he has to wait for a meal, and if I'm occupied…'

Araminta promised cold meat and a salad and went to her room to brood over her wardrobe. It was early autumn. Too late in the year for a summer outfit and too warm still for her good jacket and skirt. It would have to be the jersey two-piece with the corn silk tee shirt.

Her mother, an old-fashioned woman in many respects, considered it ladylike, which it was. It also did nothing for Araminta, who was a girl with no looks worth glancing at twice. She had mousy hair, long and fine, worn in an untidy pile on top of her head, an unremarkable face—except for large, thickly fringed hazel eyes—and a nicely rounded person, largely unnoticed since her clothes had always been chosen with an eye to their suitability.

They were always in sensible colours, in fabrics not easily spoilt by small sticky fingers which would go to the cleaners or the washing machine time and time again. She studied her reflection in the looking glass and sighed over her small sharp nose and wide mouth.

She had a lovely smile, but since she had no reason to smile at her own face she was unaware of that.

Not that that mattered; this uncle would probably be a prosey old bachelor, and, since he was a friend of Dr Jenkell, of a similar age.

She was up early the following morning to take tea to her parents, give Cherub his breakfast and tidy the house, put lunch ready and then catch the bus to Henley.

A little over two hours later she was walking along a narrow street close to Cavendish Square. It was very quiet, with tall Regency houses on either side of it, their paintwork pristine, brass doorknockers gleaming. Whoever uncle was, reflected Araminta, he had done well for himself.

The house she was looking for was at the end of the terrace, with an alley beside it leading to mews behind the houses. Delightful, reflected Araminta, and she banged the knocker.

The man who answered the door was short and thin with sandy hair, small dark eyes and a very sharp nose. Just like a rat, thought Araminta, and added, a nice rat, for he had a friendly smile and the little eyes twinkled.

It was only then that she perceived that she should have made an appointment; uncle was probably out on his rounds—did doctors who lived in grand houses have rounds? She didn't allow herself to be discouraged by the thought.

'I would like to see Dr van der Breugh. I should

have made an appointment but it's really rather urgent. It concerns his two nephews…'

'Ah, yes, miss. If you would wait while I see if the doctor is free.'

He led the way down a narrow hall and opened a door. His smile was friendly. 'I won't be two ticks,' he assured her. 'Make yourself comfortable.'

The moment he had closed the door behind him, she got up from her chair and began a tour of the room. It was at the back of the house and the windows, tall and narrow, overlooked a small walled garden with the mews beyond. It was furnished with a pleasant mixture of antique cabinets, tables and two magnificent sofas on either side of an Adam fireplace. There were easy chairs, too, and a vast mirror over the fireplace. A comfortable room, even if rather grand, and obviously used, for there was a dog basket by one of the windows and a newspaper thrown down on one of the tables.

She studied her person in the mirror, something which brought her no satisfaction. The jersey two-piece, in a sensible brown, did nothing for her, and her hair had become a little ruffled. She poked at it impatiently and then looked round guiltily as the door opened.

'If you will come this way, miss,' said the rat-faced man. 'The boss has got ten minutes to spare.'

Was he the butler? she wondered, following him out of the room. If so, he wasn't very respectful. Perhaps modern butlers had freedom of speech…

They went back down the hall and he opened a door on the other side of it.

'Miss Pomfrey,' he announced, and gave her a friendly shove before shutting the door on her.

It was a fair-sized room, lined with bookshelves, one corner of it taken up by a large desk. The man sitting at it got to his feet as Araminta hesitated, staring at him. This surely couldn't be uncle. He was a giant of a man with fair hair touched with silver, a handsome man with a high-bridged nose, a thin, firm mouth and a determined chin. He took off the glasses he was wearing and smiled as he came to her and shook hands.

'Miss Pomfrey? Dr Jenkell told me that you might come and see me. No doubt you would like some details—'

'Look,' said Araminta urgently, 'before you say any more, I've come to tell you that I can't look after your nephews. I'm starting as a student nurse in two weeks' time. I didn't know about this job until Dr Jenkell told me. I'm sure he meant it kindly, and my parents thought it was a splendid idea, but they arranged it all while I wasn't there.'

The doctor pulled up a chair. 'Do sit down and tell me about it,' he invited. He had a quiet, rather slow way of speaking, and she felt soothed by it, as was intended.

'Briskett is bringing us coffee…'

Araminta forgot for the moment why she was there. She felt surprisingly comfortable with the doctor, as though she had known him for years. She said now, 'Briskett? The little man who answered the door? Is he your butler? He called you "the boss"—I mean, he doesn't talk like a butler…'

'He runs the house for me, most efficiently. His rather unusual way of talking is, I fancy, due to his addiction to American films; they represent democracy to him. Every man is an equal. Nevertheless, he is a most trustworthy and hard-working man; I've had him for years. He didn't upset you?'

'Heavens, no. I liked him. He looks like a friendly rat,' she explained. 'Beady eyes, you know, and a sharp nose. He has a lovely smile.'

Briskett came in then, with the coffee tray, which he set down on a small table near Araminta's chair. 'You be mother,' he said, and added, 'Don't you forget you've to be at the hospital, sir.'

'Thank you, Briskett, I'll be leaving very shortly.'

Asked to do so, Araminta poured their coffee. 'I'm sorry if I'm being inconvenient,' she said. 'You see, I thought if you didn't expect me it would be easier for me to explain and you wouldn't have time to argue.'

The doctor managed not to smile. He agreed gravely. 'I quite see that the whole thing is a misunderstanding and I'm sorry you have been vexed.' He added smoothly, with just a touch of regret allowed to show, 'You would have done splendidly, I feel sure. They are six years old, the boys, twins and a handful. I must find someone young and patient to cope with them. Their parents—their mother is my sister—are archaeologists and are going to the Middle East for a month or so. It seemed a good idea if the children were to make their home with me while they are away. I leave for Holland in a week's time, and if I can't find someone suitable, I'm afraid their mother will have to stay here in England. A pity, but it can't be helped.'

'If they went to Holland with you, would they live with you? I mean, don't you have a wife?'

'My dear Miss Pomfrey, I am a very busy man. I've no time to look for a wife and certainly no time to marry. I have a housekeeper and her husband, both too elderly to cope with small boys. I intend sending them to morning school and shall spend as much time with them as I can, but they will need someone to look after them.'

He put down his coffee cup. 'I'm sorry you had to come and see me, but I quite understand that you are committed. Though I feel that we should all have got on splendidly together.'

She was being dismissed very nicely. She got up. 'Yes, I think we would too. I'm sorry. I'll go—or you'll be late at the hospital.'

She held out a hand and had it taken in his large, firm clasp. To her utter surprise she heard herself say, 'If I cancelled my place at the hospital, do you suppose they'd let me apply again? It's St Jules'...'

'I have a clinic there. I have no doubt that they

would allow that. There is always a shortage of student nurses.'

'And how long would I be in Holland?'

'Oh, a month, six weeks—perhaps a little longer. But you mustn't think of altering your plans just to oblige me, Miss Pomfrey.'

'I'm not obliging you,' said Araminta, not beating about the bush. 'I would like to look after the boys, if you think I'd do.' She studied his face; he looked grave but friendly. 'I've no idea why I've changed my mind,' she told him, 'but I've waited so long to start my training as a nurse, another month or two really won't matter.' She added anxiously, 'I won't be too old, will I? To start training…?'

'I should imagine not. How old are you?'

'Twenty-three.'

'You aren't too old,' he assured her in a kind voice, 'and if it will help you at all, I'll see if I can get you on to the next take-in once you are back in England.'

'Now that would be kind of you. Will you let me know when you want me and how I'm to get to Holland? I'm going now; you'll be late and Briskett will hate me.'

He laughed then. 'Somehow I think not. I'll be in touch.'

He went into the hall with her and Briskett was there, too.

'Cutting it fine,' he observed severely. He opened the door for Araminta. 'Go carefully,' he begged her.

*   *   *

Araminta got on a bus for Oxford Street, found a café and over a cup of coffee sorted out her thoughts. That she was doing something exactly opposite to her intentions was a fact which she bypassed for the moment. She had, with a few impulsive words, rearranged her future. A future about which she knew almost nothing, too.

Where exactly was she to go? How much would she be paid? What about free time? The language question? The doctor had mentioned none of these. Moreover, he had accepted her decision without surprise and in a casual manner which, when she thought about it, annoyed her. He should be suitably grateful that she had delayed her plans to accommodate his. She had another cup of coffee and a bun and thought about clothes.

She had a little money of her own. In theory she kept the small salary she had been getting at the convalescent home to spend as she wished, but in practice she used it to bolster up the housekeeping money her father gave her each month.

Neither he nor her mother were interested in how it was spent. The mundane things of life—gas bills, the plumber, the most economical cuts of meat— meant nothing to them; they lived in their own world of the Celts, who, to them at least, were far more important and interesting.

Now she must spend some of her savings on clothes. She wouldn't need much: a jacket, which would stand up to rain, a skirt and one or two wool-

lies, and shoes—the sensible pair she wore to the convalescent home were shabby. No need for a new
dress; she wasn't likely to go anywhere.

And her parents; someone would have to keep an
eye on them if she were to go to Holland in a week's
time and if Aunt Millicent, the elderly cousin, was
unable to come earlier than they had arranged. Mrs
Snow in the village might oblige for a few days, with
basic cooking and cleaning. Really, she thought vexedly, she could make no plans until she heard from
Dr van der Breugh.

Her parents received her news with mild interest.
Her mother nodded her head in a knowledgeable way
and observed that both she and Araminta's father
knew what was best for her and she was bound to
enjoy herself, as well as learn something of a foreign
land, even if it was only a very small one like
Holland. She added that she was sure that Araminta
would arrange everything satisfactorily before she
went. 'You'll like looking after the dear little boys.'

Araminta said that, yes, she expected she would.
Probably they were as tiresome and grubby as all
small boys, but she was fond of children and had no
qualms about the job. She would have even less when
she knew more about it.

A state of affairs which was put right the next
morning, when she received a letter from Dr van der
Breugh. It was a long letter, typed, and couched in
businesslike language. She would be called for at her
home on the following Sunday at eleven o'clock and

would spend a few hours with her charges before travelling to Holland on the night ferry from Harwich. She would be good enough to carry a valid passport and anything she might require overnight. It was hoped that her luggage might be confined to no more than two suitcases.

She would have a day off each week, and every evening after eight o'clock, and such free time during the day as could be arranged. Her salary would be paid to her weekly in Dutch guldens… She paused here to do some arithmetic—she considered it a princely sum, which certainly sweetened the somewhat arbitrary tone of the letter. Although there was no reason why it should have been couched in friendlier terms; she scarcely knew the doctor and didn't expect to see much of him while she was in Holland.

She told her mother that the arrangements for her new job seemed quite satisfactory, persuaded Mrs Snow to undertake the housekeeping until Aunt Millicent could come, and then sifted through her wardrobe. The jersey two-piece and the corn silk blouse, an equally sober skirt and an assortment of tops and a warmer woolly or two, a short wool jacket to go over everything and a perfectly plain dress in a soft blue crêpe; an adequate choice of clothes, she considered, adding a raincoat, plain slippers and undies.

She had good shoes and a leather handbag; gloves and stockings and a headscarf or two would fill the odd corners in the one case she intended taking. Her overnight bag would take the rest. She liked clothes, but working in the children's convalescent home had called for sensible skirts and tops in sensible colours, and she had seldom had much of a social life. She was uneasily aware that her clothes were dull, but there was no time to change that, and anyway, she hadn't much money. Perhaps she would get a new outfit in Holland…

The week went quickly. She cleaned and polished, washed and ironed, laid in a stock of food and got a room ready for Aunt Millicent. And she went into Henley and bought new shoes, low-heeled brown leather and expensive, and when she saw a pink angora sweater in a shop window she bought that too. She was in two minds about buying a new jacket, but caution took over then. She had already spent more money than she'd intended. Though caution wasn't quite strong enough to prevent her buying a pretty silk blouse which would render the sober skirt less sober.

On Sunday morning she was ready and waiting by eleven o'clock—waiting with her parents who, despite their wish to get back to researching the Ancient Celts, had come into the hall to see her off. Cherub was there too, looking morose, and she stooped to give him a final hug; they would miss each other.

Exactly on the hour a car drew up outside and Briskett got out, wished them all good morning, stowed her case in the boot and held the rear car door open for her.

'Oh, I'd rather sit in front with you,' said Araminta, and she gave her parents a final kiss before getting into the car, waved them a cheerful goodbye and sat back beside Briskett. It was a comfortable car, a Jaguar, and she could see from the moment Briskett took the wheel that despite his unlikely looks they hid the soul of a born driver.

There wasn't much traffic until they reached Henley and here Briskett took the road to Oxford.

'Aren't I to go to the London address?' asked Araminta.

'No, miss. The doctor thought it wise if you were to make the acquaintance of the boys at their home. They live with their parents at Oxford. The doctor will come for you and them later today and drive to Harwich for the night ferry.'

'Oh, well, I expect that's a good idea. Are you coming to Holland too?'

'No, miss. I'll stay to keep an eye on things here; the boss has adequate help in Holland. He's for ever to-ing and fro-ing—having two homes, as it were.'

'Then why can't the two boys stay here in England?'

'He'll be in Holland for a few weeks, popping over here when he is needed. Much in demand, he is.'

'We won't be expected to pop over, too? Very un-settling for the little boys...'

'Oh, no, miss. That's why you've been engaged; he can come and go without being hampered, as you might say.'

The house he stopped before in Oxford was in a terrace of similar comfortably large houses, standing well back from the road. Araminta got out and stood beside Briskett in the massive porch waiting for someone to answer the bell. She was a self-contained girl, not given to sudden bursts of excitement, but she was feeling nervous now.

Supposing the boys disliked her on sight? It was possible. Or their parents might not like the look of her. After all, they knew nothing about her, and now that she came to think about it, nor did Dr van der Breugh. But she didn't allow these uncertain feelings to show; the door was opened by a girl in a pinafore, looking harassed, and she and Briskett went into the hall.

'Miss Pomfrey,' said Briskett. 'She's expected.'

The girl nodded and led them across the hall and into a large room overlooking a garden at the back of the house. It was comfortably furnished, extremely untidy, and there were four people in it. The man and woman sitting in easy chairs with the Sunday papers strewn around them got up.

The woman was young and pretty, tall and slim, and well dressed in casual clothes. She came to meet Araminta as she hesitated by the door.

'Miss Pomfrey, how nice of you to come all this way. We're so grateful. I'm Lucy Ingram, Marcus's sister—but of course you know that—and this is my husband, Jack.'

Araminta shook hands with her and then with Mr

Ingram, a rather short stout man with a pleasant rugged face, while his wife spoke to Briskett, who left the room with a cheerful, 'So long, miss, I'll see you later.'

'Such a reliable man, and so devoted to Marcus,' said his sister. 'Come and meet the boys.'

They were at the other end of the room, sitting at a small table doing a jigsaw puzzle, unnaturally and suspiciously quiet. They were identical twins which, reflected Araminta, wasn't going to make things any easier, and they looked too good to be true.

'Peter and Paul,' said their mother. 'If you look carefully you'll see that Peter has a small scar over his right eye. He fell out of a tree years ago—it makes it easy to tell them apart.'

She beckoned them over and they came at once, two seemingly angelic children. Araminta wondered what kind of a bribe they had been offered to behave so beautifully. She shook their small hands in turn and smiled.

'Hello,' she said. 'You'll have to help me to tell you apart, and you mustn't mind if I muddle you up at first.'

'I'm Peter. What's your name—not Miss Pomfrey, your real name?'

'Araminta.'

The boys looked at each other. 'That's a long name.'

They cast their mother a quick look. 'We'll call you Mintie.'

'That's not very polite,' began Mrs Ingram.

'If you've no objection, I think it's a nice idea. I don't feel a bit like Miss Pomfrey…'

'Well, if you don't mind—go and have your milk, boys, while we have our coffee and then you can show Miss…Mintie your room and get to know each other a bit.'

They went away obediently, eyeing her as they went, and Araminta was led to a sofa and given coffee while she listened to Mrs Ingram's friendly chatter. From time to time her husband spoke, asking her quietly about her work at the children's home and if she had ever been to Holland before.

'The boys,' he told her forthrightly, 'can be little demons, but I dare say you are quite used to that. On the whole they're decent kids, and they dote on their uncle.'

Araminta, considering this remark, thought that probably it would be quite easy to dote on him, although, considering the terseness of his letter to her, not very rewarding. She would have liked to get to know him, but common sense told her that that was unlikely. Besides, once she was back in England again, he would be consigned to an easily forgotten past and she would have embarked on her nursing career…

She dismissed her thoughts and listened carefully to Mrs Ingram's instructions about the boys' clothing and meals.

'I'm telling you all these silly little details,' explained Mrs Ingram, 'because Marcus won't want to be bothered with them.' She looked anxious. 'I hope you won't find it too much…'

Araminta made haste to assure her that that was unlikely. 'At the children's home we had about forty children, and I'm used to them—two little boys will be delightful. They don't mind going to Holland?'

'No. I expect they'll miss us for a few days, but they've been to their uncle's home before, so they won't feel strange.'

Mrs Ingram began to ask carefully polite questions about Araminta and she answered them readily. If she had been Mrs Ingram she would have done the same, however well recommended she might be. Dr van der Breugh had engaged her on Dr Jenkell's advice, which was very trusting of him. Certainly he hadn't bothered with delving into her personal background.

They had lunch presently and she was pleased to see that the boys behaved nicely at the table and weren't finicky about their food. All the same, she wondered if these angelic manners would last. If they were normal little boys they wouldn't…

The rest of the day she spent with them, being shown their toys and taken into the garden to look at the goldfish in the small pond there, and their behaviour was almost too good to be true. There would be a reason for it, she felt sure; time enough to discover that during the new few weeks.

They answered her questions politely but she took

care not to ask too many. To them she was a stranger, and she would have to earn their trust and friendship.

They went indoors presently and found Dr van der Breugh in the drawing room with their father and mother. There was no doubt that they were fond of him and that he returned the affection. Emerging from their boisterous greeting, he looked across at Araminta and bade her good afternoon.

'We shall be leaving directly after tea, Miss Pomfrey. My sister won't mind if you wish to phone your mother.'

'Thank you, I should like to do that…'

'She's not Miss Pomfrey,' said Peter. 'She's Mintie.'

'Indeed?' He looked amused. 'You have rechristened her?'

'Well, of course we have, Uncle. Miss Pomfrey isn't *her*, is it? Miss Pomfrey would be tall and thin, with a sharp nose and a wart and tell us not to get dirty. Mintie's nice; she's not pretty, but she smiles…'

Araminta had gone a bright pink and his mother said hastily, 'Hush, dear. Miss Pomfrey, come with me and I'll show you where you can phone.'

Leading Araminta across the hall, she said apologetically, 'I do apologise. Peter didn't mean to be rude—indeed, I believe he was paying you a compliment.'

Araminta laughed. 'Well, I'm glad they think of

me as Mintie, and not some tiresome woman with a wart. I hope we're going to like each other.'

The boys had been taken upstairs to have their hands washed and the two men were alone.

'Good of you to have the boys,' said Mr Ingram. 'Lucy was getting in a bit of a fret. And this treasure you've found for them seems just like an answer to a prayer. Quiet little thing and, as Peter observed, not pretty, but a nice calm voice. I fancy she'll do. Know much about her?'

'Almost nothing. Old Jenkell told me of her; he's known her almost all her life. He told me that she was entirely trustworthy, patient and kind. They loved her at the children's home. She didn't want to come— she was to start her training as a nurse in a week or so—but she changed her mind after refusing the job. I don't know why. I've said I'll help her to get into the next batch of students when we get back.'

The doctor wandered over to the windows. 'You'll miss your garden.' He glanced over his shoulder. 'I'll keep an eye on the boys, Jack. As you say, I think we have found a treasure in Miss Pomfrey. A nice, unassuming girl who won't intrude. Which suits me very well.'

Tea was a proper meal, taken at the table since the boys ate with them, but no time was wasted on it. Farewells were said, the boys were settled by their uncle in the back seat of his Bentley, and Araminta got into the front of the car, composed and very neat. The doctor, turning to ask her if she was comfortable, allowed himself a feeling of satisfaction. She was indeed unassuming, both in manner and appearance.

CHAPTER TWO

ARAMINTA, happily unaware of the doctor's opinion of her, settled back in the comfort of the big car, but she was aware of his voice keeping up a steady flow of talk with his little nephews. He sounded cheerful, and from the occasional words she could hear he was talking about sailing. Would she be expected to take part in this sport? she wondered. She hoped not, but, being a sensible girl, she didn't allow the prospect to worry her. Whatever hazards lay ahead they would be for a mere six weeks or so. The salary was generous and she was enjoying her freedom. She felt guilty about that, although she knew that her parents would be perfectly happy with Aunt Millicent.

The doctor drove through Maidenhead and on to Slough and then, to her surprise, instead of taking the ring road to the north of London, he drove to his house.

Araminta, who hadn't seen Briskett leave the Ingrams', was surprised to see him open the door to them.

'Right on time,' he observed. 'Not been travelling over the limit, I hope, sir. You lads wait there while I see to Miss Pomfrey. There's a couple of phone calls for you, Doc.'

He led Araminta to the cloakroom at the back of the hall. 'You tidy yourself, miss; I'll see to the boys. There's coffee ready in the drawing room.'

Araminta, not in the least untidy, nonetheless did as she was bid. Briskett, for all his free and easy ways, was a gem. He would be a handy man in a crisis.

When she went back into the hall he was there, waiting to usher her into the drawing room. The doctor was already there, leaning over a sofa table with the boys, studying a map. He straightened up as she went in and offered her a chair and asked her to pour their coffee. There was milk for the boys as well as a plate of biscuits and a dish of sausage rolls, which Peter and Paul demolished.

They were excited now, their sadness at leaving their mother and father already fading before the prospect of going to bed on board the ferry. Presently the doctor excused himself with the plea that there were phone calls he must make and Araminta set to work to calm them down, something at which she was adept. By the time their uncle came back they were sitting quietly beside her, listening to her telling them a story.

He paused in the doorway. 'I think it might be a good idea if you sat in the back with the boys in the car, Miss Pomfrey...'

'Mintie,' said Peter. 'Uncle Marcus, she's Mintie.'

'Mintie,' said the doctor gravely. 'If Miss Pomfrey does not object?'

'Not a bit,' said Araminta cheerfully.

They left shortly after that, crossing London in the comparative calm of a Sunday evening, onto the A12, through Brentford, Chelmsford, Colchester and finally to Harwich. Long before they had reached the port the two boys were asleep, curled up against Araminta. She sat, rather warm and cramped, with an arm around each of them, watching the doctor driving. He was a good driver.

She reflected that he would be an interesting man to know. It was a pity that the opportunity to do that was improbable. She wondered why he wasn't married and allowed her imagination to roam. A widower? A love affair which had gone wrong and left him with a broken heart and dedicated to his work? Engaged? The last was the most likely. She had a sudden urge to find out.

They were amongst the last to go on board, and the doctor with one small sleeping boy and a porter with the other led the way to their cabins.

Araminta was to share a cabin with the boys; it was roomy and comfortable and well furnished, with a shower room, and once her overnight bag and the boys' luggage had been brought to her she lost no time in undressing them and popping them into their narrow beds. They roused a little, but once tucked up slept again. She unpacked her night things and wondered what she should do. Would the doctor mind if she rang for a pot of tea and a sandwich? It was almost midnight and she was hungry.

A tap on the door sent her to open it and find him outside.

'A stewardess will keep an eye on the boys. Come and have a meal; it will give me the opportunity to outline your day's work.'

She was only too glad to agree to that; she went with him to the restaurant and made a splendid supper while she listened to him quietly describing the days ahead.

'I live in Utrecht. The house is in the centre of the city, but there are several parks close by and I have arranged for the boys to attend school in the mornings. You will be free then, but I must ask you to be with them during the rest of the day. You will know best how to keep them happy and entertained.

'I have a housekeeper and a houseman who will do all they can to make life easy for you and them. When I am free I will have the boys with me. I am sure that you will want to do some sightseeing. I expect my sister has told you her wishes concerning their clothes and daily routine. I must warn you that they are as naughty as the average small boy...they are also devoted to each other.'

Araminta speared a morsel of grilled sole. 'I'll do the best I can to keep them happy and content, Dr van der Breugh. And I shall come to you if I have any problems. You will be away during the day? Working? Will I know where you are?'

'Yes, I will always leave a phone number for you or a message with Bas. He speaks English of a sort, and is very efficient.' He smiled at her kindly. 'I'm sure everything will be most satisfactory, Miss Pomfrey. And now I expect you would like to go to your bed. You will be called in good time in the morning. We will see how the boys are then. If they're too excited to eat breakfast we will stop on the way and have something, but there should be time for a meal before we go ashore. You can manage them and have them up and ready?'

Araminta assured him that she could. Several years in the convalescent home had made her quite sure about that. She thanked him for her dinner, wished him goodnight, and was surprised when he went back to her cabin with her and saw her into it.

Nice manners, thought Araminta, getting undressed as fast as she could, having a quick shower and jumping into her bed after a last look at the boys—deeply asleep.

The boys woke when the stewardess brought morning tea. They drank the milk in the milk jug and ate all the biscuits. Talking non-stop, they washed and cleaned their teeth and dressed after a fashion. Araminta was tying shoelaces and inspecting fingernails when there was a knock on the door and the doctor came in.

'If anyone is hungry there's plenty of time for breakfast,' he observed. He looked at Araminta. 'You all slept well?'

'Like logs,' she told him, 'and we're quite ready, with everything packed.'

'Splendid. Come along, then.' He sounded briskly cheerful and she wondered if he found this disruption in his ordered life irksome. If he did, he didn't allow it to show. Breakfast was a cheerful meal, eaten without waste of time since they were nearing the Hoek of Holland and the boys wanted to see the ferry dock.

Disembarking took time, but finally they were away from the customs shed, threading their way through the town.

'We'll go straight home,' said the doctor. He had the two boys with him again and spoke to Araminta over his shoulder. 'Less than an hour's drive.' He picked up the car phone and spoke into it. 'I've told them we are on our way.'

There was a great deal of traffic as they neared Rotterdam, where they drove through the long tunnel under the Maas. Once through it, the traffic was even heavier. But presently, as they reached the outskirts of the city and were once more on the motorway, it thinned, and Araminta was able to look about her.

The country was flat, and she had expected that, but it was charming all the same, with farms well away from the highway, small copses of trees already turning to autumn tints, green meadows separated by narrow canals, and cows and horses roaming freely. The motorway bypassed the villages and towns, but she caught tantalising glimpses of them from time to time and promised herself that if she should get any free time, she would explore away from the main roads.

As though he had read her thoughts, the doctor said over his shoulder, 'This is dull, isn't it? But it's the quickest way home. Before you go back we must try and show you some of rural Holland. I think you might like it.'

She murmured her thanks. 'It's a very good road,' she said politely, anxious not to sound disparaging.

'All the motorways are good. Away from them it's a different matter. But you will see for yourself.'

Presently he turned off into a narrow country road between water meadows. 'We're going to drive along the River Vecht. It is the long way round to Utrecht, but well worth it. It will give you a taste of rural Holland.'

He drove north, away from Utrecht, and then turned into another country road running beside a river lined with lovely old houses set in well-kept grounds.

'The East Indies merchants built their houses here—there's rather a splendid castle you'll see presently on your right. There are a number in Utrecht province—most of them privately owned. You must find time to visit one of those open to the public before you go back to England.'

Apparently satisfied that he had given her enough to go on with, he began a lively conversation with the boys, leaving her to study her surroundings. They were certainly charming, but she had the feeling that he had offered the information in much the same manner as a dutiful and well mannered host would offer a drink to an unexpected and tiresome guest.

They were on the outskirts of Utrecht by now, and soon at its heart. Some magnificent buildings, she conceded, and a bewildering number of canals. She glimpsed several streets of shops, squares lined by tall, narrow houses with gabled roofs and brief views of what she supposed were parks.

The boys were talking now, nineteen to the dozen, and in Dutch. Well, of course, they would, reflected Araminta. They had a Dutch mother and uncle. They were both talking at once, interrupted from time to time by the doctor's measured tones, but presently Paul shouted over his shoulder, 'We're here, Mintie. Do look, isn't it splendid?'

She looked. They were in a narrow *gracht*, tree-lined, with houses on either side of the canal in all shapes and sizes: some of them crooked with age, all with a variety of gabled roofs. The car had stopped at the end of the *gracht* before a narrow red-brick house with double steps leading up to its solid door. She craned her neck to see its height—four storeys, each with three windows. The ground floor ones were large, but they got progressively smaller at each storey so that the top ones of all were tucked in between the curve of the gable.

The doctor got out, went around to allow the boys to join him and then opened her door. He said kindly, 'I hope you haven't found the journey too tiring?'

Araminta said, 'Not in the least,' and felt as elderly

as his glance indicated. Probably she looked twice her age; her toilet on board had been sketchy…

The boys had run up the steps, talking excitedly to the man who had opened the door, and the doctor, gently urging her up the steps said, 'This is Bas, who runs my home with his wife. As I said, he speaks English, and will do all he can to help you.'

She offered a hand and smiled at the elderly lined face with its thatch of grey hair. Bas shook hands and said gravely, 'We welcome you, miss, and shall do our best to make you happy.'

Which was nice, she thought, and wished that the doctor had said something like that.

What he did say was rather absent-minded. 'Yes, yes, Miss Pomfrey. Make yourself at home and ask Bas for anything you may need.'

Which she supposed was the next best thing to a welcome.

The hall they entered was long and narrow, with a great many doors on either side of it, and halfway along it there was a staircase, curving upwards between the panelled walls. As they reached a pair of magnificent mahogany doors someone came to meet them from the back of the house. It was a short, stout woman in a black dress and wearing a printed pinny over it. She had a round rosy face and grey hair screwed into a bun. Her eyes were very dark and as she reached them she gave Araminta a quick look.

'Jet…' Dr van der Breugh sounded pleased to see her and indeed kissed her cheek and spoke at some length in his own language. His housekeeper smiled then, shook Araminta's hand and bent to hug the boys, talking all the time.

The doctor said in English, 'Go with Jet to the kitchen, both of you, and have milk and biscuits. Miss Pomfrey shall fetch you as soon as she has had a cup of coffee.'

Bas opened the doors and Araminta, invited to enter the room, did so. It was large and lofty, with two windows overlooking the *gracht*, a massive fireplace along one wall and glass doors opening into a room beyond. It was furnished with two vast sofas on either side of the fireplace and a number of comfortable chairs. There was a Pembroke table between the windows and a rosewood sofa table on which a china bowl of late roses glowed.

A walnut and marquetry display cabinet took up most of the wall beside the fireplace on one side, and on the other there was a black and gold laquer cabinet on a gilt stand. Above it was a great *stoel* clock, its quiet tick-tock somehow enhancing the peace of the room. And the furnishings were restful: dull mulberry-red and dark green, the heavy curtains at the windows matching the upholstery of the sofas and chairs. The floor was highly polished oak with Kasham silk rugs, faded with age, scattered on it.

A magnificent room, reflected Araminta, and if it had been anyone other than the doctor she would have said so. She held her tongue, however, sensing that

he would give her a polite and chilly stare at her
unasked-for praise.

He said, 'Do sit down, Miss Pomfrey. Jet shall take
you to your room when you have had coffee and then
perhaps you would see to the boys' things and arrange
some kind of schedule for their day? We could discuss that later today.'

Bas brought the coffee then, and she poured it for
them both and sat drinking it silently as the doctor
excused himself while he glanced through the piles
of letters laid beside his chair, his spectacles on his
handsome nose, oblivious of her presence.

He had indeed forgotten her for the moment, but
presently he looked up and said briskly, 'I expect you
would like to go to your room. Take the boys with
you, will you? I shall be out to lunch and I suggest
that you take the boys for a walk this afternoon. They
know where the park is and Bas will tell you anything
you may wish to know.'

He went to open the door for her and she went past
him into the hall. She would have liked a second cup
of coffee…

Bas was waiting for her and took her to the kitchen,
a semi-basement room at the back of the house. It
was nice to be greeted by cheerful shouts from the
boys and Jet's kind smile and the offer of another cup
of coffee. She sat down at the old-fashioned scrubbed
table while Bas told her that he would serve their
lunch at midday and that when they came back from

their walk he would have an English afternoon tea waiting for her.

His kind old face crinkled into a smile as he told her, 'And if you should wish to telephone your family, you are to do so—*mijnheer's* orders.'

'Oh, may I? I'll do that now, before I go to my room...'

Her mother answered the phone, expressed relief that Araminta had arrived safely and observed that there were some interesting burial mounds in the north of Holland if she should have the opportunity to see them. 'And enjoy yourself, dear,' said her parent.

Araminta, not sure whether it was the burial mounds or her job which was to give her enjoyment, assured her mother that she would do so and went in search of the boys.

Led upstairs by Jet, with the boys running ahead, she found herself in a charming room on the second floor. It overlooked the street below and was charmingly furnished, with a narrow canopied bed, a dressing table under its window and two small easy chairs flanking a small round table. The colour scheme was a mixture of pastel colours and the furniture was of some pale wood she didn't recognise. There was a large cupboard and a little door led to a bathroom. The house might be old, she thought, but the plumbing was ultra-modern. It had everything one could wish for...

The boys' room was across the narrow passage,

with another bathroom, and at the end of the passage was a room which she supposed had been a nursery, for it had a low table and small chairs round it and shelves full of toys.

She was right. The boys, both talking at once, eager to show her everything, told her that some of the toys had belonged to their uncle and his father; even his grandfather.

'We have to be careful of them,' said Paul, 'but Uncle Marcus lets us play with them when we're here.'

'Do you come here often?' asked Araminta.

'Every year with Mummy and Daddy.'

Bas came to tell them that lunch was ready, so they all trooped downstairs and, since breakfast seemed a long time ago, made an excellent meal.

The boys were still excited, and Araminta judged it a good idea to take them for the walk. She could unpack later, when they had tired themselves out.

Advised by Bas and urged on by them, she got her own jacket, buttoned them into light jackets and went out into the street. The park was five minutes' walk away, small and beautifully kept, a green haven in the centre of the city. There was a small pond, with goldfish and seats under the trees, but the boys had no intention of sitting down. When they had tired of the goldfish they insisted on showing her some of the surrounding streets.

'And we'll go to the Dom Tower,' they assured her. 'It's ever so high, and the Domkerk—that's a cathedral—and perhaps Uncle will take us to the university.'

They were all quite tired by the time they got back to the house, and Araminta was glad of the tea Bas brought to them in a small room behind the drawing room.

'*Mijnheer* will be home very shortly,' he told her, 'and will be free to have the boys with him for a while whilst you unpack. They are to have their supper at half past six.'

Which reminded her that she should have some kind of plan ready for him to approve that evening.

'It's all go,' said Araminta crossly, alone for a few moments while the boys were in the kitchen, admiring Miep—the kitchen cat—and her kittens.

She had gone to the window to look out onto the narrow garden behind the house. It was a pretty place, with narrow brick paths and small flowerbeds and a high brick wall surrounding it.

'I trust you do not find the job too tiresome for you?' asked the doctor gently.

She spun round. He was standing quite close to her, looking amused.

She said tartly, 'I was talking to myself, doctor, unaware that anyone was listening. And I do not find the boys tiresome but it has been a long day.

'Indeed it has.' He didn't offer sympathy, merely agreed with her in a civil voice which still held the thread of amusement.

He glanced at his watch. 'I dare say you wish to

unpack for the boys and yourself. I'll have them with me until half past six.'

He gave her a little nod and held the door open for her.

In her room, she put away her clothes, reflecting that she must remember not to voice her thoughts out loud. He could have been nasty about it—he could also have offered a modicum of sympathy...

She still wasn't sure why she had accepted this job. True, she was to be paid a generous salary, and she supposed that she had felt sorry for him.

Upon reflection she thought that being sorry for him was a waste of time; it was apparent that he lived in some comfort, surrounded by people devoted to him. She supposed, too, that he was a busy man, although she had no idea what he did. A GP, perhaps? But his lifestyle was a bit grand for that. A consultant in one of the hospitals? Or one of those unseen men who specialised in obscure illnesses? She would find out.

She went to the boys' room and unpacked, put everything ready for bedtime and then got out pen and paper and wrote out the rough outline of a routine for the boys' day. Probably the doctor wouldn't approve of it, in which case he could make his own suggestions.

At half past six she went downstairs and found the boys in the small room where they had their tea earlier. The doctor was there, too, and they were all on the floor playing a noisy game of cards. There was a dog there too, a black Labrador, sitting beside his master, watching the cards being flung down and picked up.

They all looked up as she went in and the doctor said, 'Five minutes, Miss Pomfrey.' When the dog got to its feet and came towards her, he added, 'This is Humphrey. You like dogs?'

'Yes.' She offered a fist and then stroked the great head. 'He's lovely.'

She sat down until the game came to an end, with Peter declared the winner.

'Supper?' asked Araminta mildly.

The doctor got on to his feet, towering over them. 'Come and say goodnight when you're ready for bed. Off you go, there's good fellows.'

Bas was waiting in the hall. 'Supper is to be in the day nursery on the first floor,' he explained. 'You know the way, miss.' And they all went upstairs and into the large room, so comfortably furnished with an eye to a child's comfort.

'Uncle Marcus used to have his supper here,' Paul told her, 'and he says one day, when he's got some boys of his own, they'll have their supper here, too.'

Was the doctor about to marry? Araminta wondered. He wasn't all that young—well into his thirties, she supposed. It was high time he settled down. It would be a pity to waste this lovely old house and this cosy nursery…

Bas came in with a tray followed by a strapping girl with a round face and fair hair who grinned at them and set the table. Supper was quickly eaten, milk was drunk and Araminta whisked the boys upstairs, for they were tired now and suddenly a little unhappy.

'Are Mummy and Daddy going a long way away?' asked Peter as she bathed them.

'Well, it would be a long way if you had to walk there,' said Araminta, 'but in an aeroplane it takes no time at all to get there and get back again. Shall we buy postcards tomorrow and write to them?'

She talked cheerfully as she popped them into their pyjamas and dressing gowns and they all went back downstairs, this time to the drawing room, where their uncle was sitting with a pile of papers on the table beside him.

He hugged them, teased them gently, told them he would see them at breakfast in the morning and bade them goodnight. As they went, he reminded Araminta that dinner would be in half an hour.

The boys were asleep within minutes. Araminta had a quick shower and got into another skirt and a pretty blouse, spent the shortest possible time over her face and hair and nipped downstairs again with a few minutes to spare. She suspected that the doctor was a man who invited punctuality.

He was in the drawing room still, but he got up as she went in, offered her a glass of sherry, enquired if the boys were asleep and made small talk until Bas came to tell them that dinner was ready.

Araminta was hungry and Jet was a splendid cook.

She made her way through mushrooms in a garlic and cream sauce, roast guinea fowl, and apple tart with whipped cream. Mindful of good manners, she sustained a polite conversation the while.

The doctor, making suitable replies to her painstaking efforts allowed his thoughts to wander.

After this evening he would feel free to spend his evenings with friends or at the hospital; breakfast wasn't a problem, for the boys would be there, and he was almost always out for lunch. Miss Pomfrey was a nice enough girl, but there was nothing about her to arouse his interest. He had no doubt that she would be excellent with the boys, and she was a sensible girl who would know how to amuse herself on her days off.

Dinner over, he suggested that they had their coffee in the drawing room.

'If you don't mind,' said Araminta, 'I'd like to go to bed. I've written down the outlines of a day's schedule, if you would look at it and let me know in the morning if it suits you. Do we have breakfast with you or on our own?'

'With me. At half past seven, since I leave for the hospital soon after eight o'clock.'

Araminta nodded. 'Oh, I wondered where you worked,' she observed, and wished him goodnight.

The doctor, politely opening the door for her, had the distinct feeling that he had been dismissed.

He could find no fault with her schedule for the boys. He could see that if she intended to carry it out to the letter she would be tired by the end of the day, but that, he felt, was no concern of his. She would have an hour or so each morning while the boys were at school and he would tell her that she could have her day off during the week as long as it didn't interfere with his work.

He went back to his chair and began to read the patients' notes that he had brought with him from the hospital. There was a good deal of work waiting for him both at Utrecht and Leiden. He was an acknowledged authority on endocrinology, and there were a number of patients about which he was to be consulted. He didn't give Araminta another thought.

Araminta took her time getting ready for bed. She took a leisurely bath, and spent time searching for lines and wrinkles in her face; someone had told her that once one had turned twenty, one's skin would start to age. But since she had a clear skin, as soft as a peach, she found nothing to worry her. She got into bed, glanced at the book and magazines someone had thoughtfully put on her bedside table and decided that instead of reading she would lie quietly and sort out her thoughts. She was asleep within minutes.

A small, tearful voice woke her an hour later. Paul was standing by her bed, in tears, and a moment later Peter joined him.

Araminta jumped out of bed. 'My dears, have you had a nasty dream? Look, I'll come to your room and sit with you and you can tell me all about it. Bad dreams go away if you talk about them, you know.'

It wasn't bad dreams; they wanted their mother and father, their own home, the cat and her kittens, the goldfish... She sat down on one of the beds and settled the pair of them, one on each side of her, cuddling them close.

'Well, of course you miss them, my dears, but you'll be home again in a few weeks. Think of seeing them all again and telling them about Holland. And you've got your uncle...'

'And you, Mintie, you won't go away?'

'Gracious me, no. I'm in a foreign country, aren't I? Where would I go? I'm depending on both of you to take me round Utrecht so that I can tell everyone at home all about it.'

'Have you got little boys?' asked Peter.

'No, love, just a mother and father and a few aunts and uncles. I haven't any brothers and sisters, you see.'

Paul said in a watery voice, 'Shall we be your brothers? Just while you're living with us?'

'Oh, yes, please. What a lovely idea...'

'I heard voices,' said the doctor from the doorway. 'Bad dreams?'

Peter piped up, 'We woke up and we wanted to go home, but Mintie has explained so it's all right, Uncle, because she'll be here with you, and she says we can be her little brothers. She hasn't got a brother or a sister.'

The doctor came into the room and sat down on the other bed. 'What a splendid idea. We must think of so many things to do that we shan't have enough days in which to do them.'

He began a soothing monologue, encompassing a visit to some old friends in Friesland, another to the lakes north of Utrecht, where he had a yacht, and a shopping expedition so that they might buy presents to take home…

The boys listened, happy once more and getting sleepy. Araminta listened too, quite forgetting that she was barefoot, somewhere scantily clad in her nightie and that her hair hung round her shoulders and tumbled untidily down her back.

The doctor had given her an all-seeing look and hadn't looked again. He was a kind man, and he knew that the prim Miss Pomfrey, caught unawares in her nightie, would be upset and probably hate him just because he was there to see her looking like a normal girl. She had pretty hair, he reflected.

'Now, how about bed?' he wanted to know. 'I'm going downstairs again but I'll come up in ten minutes, so mind you're asleep by then.'

He ruffled their hair and took himself off without a word or a look for Araminta. It was only as she was tucking the boys up once more that she realised that she hadn't stopped to put on her dressing gown. She kissed the boys goodnight and went away to swathe herself in that garment now, and tie her hair back with a ribbon. She would have to see that man again, she thought vexedly, because the boys had said they wouldn't go to sleep unless she was there, but this time she would be decently covered.

He came presently, to find the boys asleep already and Araminta sitting very upright in a chair by the window.

'They wanted me to stay,' she told him, and he nodded carelessly, barely glancing at her. Perhaps he hadn't noticed, she thought, for he looked at her as though he hadn't really seen her. She gave a relieved sigh. Her, 'Goodnight, doctor,' was uttered in Miss Pomfrey's voice, and he wished her a quiet goodnight in return, amused at the sight of her swathed in her sensible, shapeless dressing gown. Old Jenkell had told him that she was the child of elderly and self-absorbed parents, who hadn't moved with the times. It seemed likely that they had not allowed her to move with them either.

Nonetheless, she was good with the boys, and so far had made no demands concerning herself. Give her a day or two, he reflected, and she would have settled down and become nothing but a vague figure in the background of his busy life.

His hopes were borne out in the morning; at breakfast she sat between the boys, and after the exchange of good mornings, neither she nor they tried to distract him from the perusal of his post.

Presently he said, 'Your schedule seems very satisfactory, Miss Pomfrey. I shall be home around tea-time. I'll take the boys with me when I take Humphrey for his evening walk. The boys start school today. You will take them, please, and fetch them at noon each day. I dare say you will enjoy an hour or so to go shopping or sightseeing.'

'Yes, thank you,' said Araminta.

Peter said, 'Uncle, why do you call Mintie Miss Pomfrey? She's Mintie.'

'My apologies. It shall be Mintie from now on.' He smiled, and she thought how it changed his whole handsome face. 'That is, if Mintie has no objection?'

She answered the smile. 'Not in the least.'

That was the second time he had asked her that. She had the lowering feeling that she had made so little impression upon him that nothing which they had said to each other had been interesting enough to be remembered.

CHAPTER THREE

THE boys had no objection to going to school. It was five minutes' walk from the doctor's house and in a small quiet street which they reached by crossing a bridge over the canal. Araminta handed them over to one of the teachers. Submitting to their hugs, she promised that she would be there at the end of the morning, and walked back to the house, where she told Bas that she would go for a walk and look around.

She found the Domkerk easily enough, but she didn't go inside; the boys had told her that they would take her there. Instead she went into a church close by, St Pieterskerk, which was Gothic with a crypt and frescoes. By the time she had wandered around, looking her fill, it was time to fetch the boys. Tomorrow she promised herself that she would go into one of the museums and remember to have coffee somewhere...

The boys had enjoyed their morning. They told her all about it as they walked back, and then demanded to know what they were going to do that afternoon.

'Well, what about buying postcards and stamps and writing to your mother and father? If you know the way, you can show me where the post office is. If you show me a different bit of Utrecht each day I'll know my way around, so that if ever I should come again...'

'Oh, I 'spect you will, Mintie,' said Paul. 'Uncle Marcus will invite you.'

Araminta thought this highly unlikely, but she didn't say so. 'That would be nice,' she said cheerfully. 'Let's have lunch while you tell me some more about school.'

The afternoon was nicely filled in by their walk to the post office and a further exploration of the neighbouring streets while the boys, puffed up with self-importance, explained about the *grachten* and the variety of gables, only too pleased to air their knowledge. They were back in good time for tea, and when Bas opened the door to them they were making a considerable noise, since Araminta had attempted to imitate the Dutch words they were intent on teaching her.

A door in the hall opened and the doctor came out. He had his spectacles on and a book in his hand and he looked coldly annoyed.

Araminta hushed the boys. 'Oh, dear, we didn't know you were home. If we had we would have been as quiet as mice.'

'I am relieved to hear that, Miss Pomfrey. I hesitate to curtail your enjoyment, but I must ask you to be as quiet as possible in the house. You can, of course, let yourself go once you are in the nursery.'

She gave him a pitying look. He should marry and

have a houseful of children and become human again. He was fast becoming a dry-as-dust old bachelor. She said kindly, 'We are really sorry, aren't we, boys? We'll creep around the house and be ourselves in the nursery.' She added, 'Little boys will be little boys, you know, but I dare say you've forgotten over the years.'

She gave him a sweet smile and shooed the boys ahead of her up the stairs.

'Is Uncle Marcus cross?' asked Paul.

'No, no, of course not. You heard what he said— we may make as much noise as we like in the nursery. There's a piano there, isn't there? We'll have a concert after tea…'

The boys liked the sound of that, only Peter said slowly, 'He must have been a bit cross because he called you Miss Pomfrey.'

'Oh, he just forgot, I expect. Now, let's wash hands for tea and go down to the nursery. I dare say we shall have it there if your uncle is working.'

The doctor had indeed gone back to his study, but he didn't immediately return to his reading. He was remembering Araminta's words with a feeing of annoyance. She had implied that he was elderly, or at least middle-aged. Thirty-six wasn't old, not even middle-aged, and her remark had rankled. True, he was fair enough to concede, he hadn't the lifestyle of other men of his age, and since he wasn't married he was free to spend as much time doing his work as he wished.

As a professor of endocrinology he had an enviable reputation in his profession already, and he was perfectly content with his life. He had friends and acquaintances, his sister, of whom he was fond, and his nephews; his social life was pleasant, and from time to time he thought of marriage, but he had never met a woman with whom he wanted to share the rest of his life.

Sooner or later, he supposed, he would have to settle for second best and marry; he had choice enough. A man of no conceit, he was still aware that there were several women of his acquaintance who would be only too delighted to marry him.

He read for a time and then got up and walked through the house to the kitchen, where he told Bas to put the tea things in the small sitting room. 'And please tell Miss Pomfrey and the boys that I expect them there for tea in ten minutes.'

After tea, he reflected, they would play the noisiest game he could think of!

He smiled then, amused that the tiresome girl should have annoyed him. She hadn't meant to annoy him; he was aware of that. He had seen enough of her to know that she was a kind girl, though perhaps given to uttering thoughts best kept to herself.

Araminta, rather surprised at his message, went downstairs with the boys to find him already sitting in the chair by the open window, Humphrey at his feet. He got up as they went in and said easily, 'I thought we might as well have tea together round the table. I believe Jet has been making cakes and some of those *pofferjes* which really have to be eaten from a plate, don't they?'

He drew out a chair and said pleasantly. 'Do sit down, Miss Pomfrey.'

'Mintie,' Peter reminded him.

'Mintie,' said his uncle meekly, and Araminta gave him a wide smile, relieved that he wasn't annoyed.

Tea poured and Jet's *botorkeok* cut and served, he asked, 'Well, what have you done all day? Was school all right?'

The boys were never at a loss for words, so there was little need for Araminta to say anything, merely to agree to something when appealed to. Doubtless over dinner he would question her more closely. She would be careful to be extra polite, she thought; he was a good-natured man, and his manners were beautiful, but she suspected that he expected life to be as he arranged it and wouldn't tolerate interference. She really must remember that she was merely the governess in his employ—and in a temporary capacity. She would have to remember that, too.

They played Monopoly after tea, sitting at the table after Bas had taken the tea things away. The boys were surprisingly good at it, and with a little help and a lot of hints Peter won with Paul a close second. The doctor had taken care to make mistakes and had even cheated, although Araminta had been the only one to see that. As for her, she would never, as he had mildly pointed out, be a financial wizard.

She began to tidy up while the boys said a pro-
tracted goodnight to their uncle. 'You'll come up and
say goodnight again?' they begged.

When he agreed they went willingly enough to
their baths, their warm milk drinks with the little
sugar biscuits, and bed. Araminta, rather flushed and
untidy, was tucking them in when the doctor came
upstairs. He had changed for the evening and she silently admired him. Black tie suited him and his
clothes had been cut by a masterly hand. The blue
crêpe would be quite inadequate…

He bade the boys goodnight and then turned to her.
'I shall be out for dinner, Miss Pomfrey,' he told her
with a formal politeness which she found chilling.
'Bas will look after you. Dinner will be at the usual
time, otherwise do feel free to do whatever you wish.'

She suppressed an instant wish to go with him. To
some grand house where there would be guests? More
likely he was taking some exquisitely gowned girl to
one of those restaurants where there were little pink-
shaded table lamps and the menus were the size of a
ground map…

And she was right, for Paul asked sleepily, 'Are
you going out with a pretty lady, Uncle Marcus?'

The doctor smiled. 'Indeed I am, Paul. Tomorrow
I'll tell you what we had for dinner.'

He nodded to Araminta and went away, and she
waited, sitting quietly by the window, until she judged
that he had left the house. Of course, there was no
reason for him to stay at home to dine with her; she

had been a fool to imagine that he would do so. Good manners had obliged him to do so yesterday, since it had been her first evening there, but it wasn't as if she was an interesting person to be with. Her mother had pointed out kindly and rather too frequently that she lacked wit and sparkle, and that since she wasn't a clever girl, able to converse upon interesting subjects, then she must be content to be a good listener.

Araminta had taken this advice in good part, knowing that her mother was unaware that she was trampling on her daughter's feelings. Araminta made allowances for her, though; people with brilliant brains were quite often careless of other people's feelings. And it was all quite true. She knew herself to be just what her mother had so succinctly described. And she had taught herself to be a good listener...

She might have had to dine alone, but Bas treated her as though she was an honoured guest and the food was delicious.

'I will put coffee in the drawing room, miss,' said Bas, so she went and sat there, with Humphrey for comfort and companionship, and presently wandered about the room, looking at the portraits on its walls and the silver and china displayed in the cabinet. It was still early—too early to go to bed. She slipped upstairs to make sure that the boys were sleeping and then went back to the drawing room and leafed through the magazines on the sofa table. But she put those down after a few minutes and curled up on one of the sofas and allowed her thoughts to wander.

The day had, on the whole, gone well. The boys liked her and she liked them, the house was beautiful and her room lacked nothing in the way of comfort. Bas and Jet were kindness itself, and Utrecht was undoubtedly a most interesting city. There was one niggling doubt: despite his concern for her comfort and civil manner towards her, she had the uneasy feeling that the doctor didn't like her. And, of course, she had made it worse, answering him back. She must keep a civil tongue in her head and remember that she was there to look after the boys. He was paying her for that, wasn't he?

'And don't forget that, my girl,' said Araminta in a voice loud enough to rouse Humphrey from his snooze.

She went off to bed then, after going to the kitchen to wish Bas and Jet goodnight, suddenly anxious not to be downstairs when the doctor came home.

He wasn't at breakfast the next morning; Bas told them that he had gone early to Amsterdam but hoped to be back in the late afternoon. The boys were disappointed and so, to her surprise, was Araminta.

He was home when they got back from their afternoon walk. The day had gone well and the boys were bursting to tell him about it, so Araminta took their caps and coats from them in the hall, made sure that they had wiped their shoes, washed their hands and combed their hair, and told them to go and find their uncle.

'You'll come, too? It's almost time for tea, Mintie.' Paul sounded anxious.

'I'll come presently, love. I'll take everything upstairs first.'

She didn't hurry downstairs. There was still ten minutes or so before Bas would take in the tea tray. She would go then, stay while the boys had their tea and then leave them with their uncle if he wished. In that way she would need only to hold the briefest of conversations with him. The thought of dining with him later bothered her, so she began to list some suitable subjects about which she could talk...

She arrived in the drawing room as Bas came with the tea things, and the doctor's casual, 'Good afternoon, Miss Pomfrey. You have had a most interesting walk, so the boys tell me,' was the cue for her to enlarge upon that. But after a moment or so she realised that she was boring him.

'The boys will have told you all this already,' she observed in her matter-of-fact way. She gave the boys their milk and handed him a cup of tea. 'I hope you had a good day yourself, doctor?'

He looked surprised. 'Yes—yes, I did. I'll keep the boys with me until their bedtime, if you would fetch them at half past six?'

There was really no need to worry about conversation; the boys had a great deal to say to their uncle, often lapsing into Dutch, and once tea was finished, she slipped away with a quiet, 'I'll be back presently.'

She put everything ready for the boys' bedtime and

then went quietly downstairs and out of the kitchen door into the garden. Jet, busy preparing dinner, smiled and nodded as she crossed the kitchen, and Araminta smiled and nodded back. There was really no need to talk, she reflected, they understood each other very well—moreover, they liked each other.

The garden was beautifully kept, full of sweet-smelling shrubs and flowers, and at its end there was a wooden seat against a brick wall, almost hidden by climbing plants. The leaves were already turning and the last of the evening sun was turning them to bronze. It was very quiet, and she sat idly, a small, lonely figure.

The doctor, looking up from the jigsaw puzzle he was working on with the boys, glanced idly out of the window and saw her sitting there. At that distance she appeared forlorn, and he wondered if she was unhappy and then dismissed the idea. Miss Pomfrey was a sensible, matter-of-fact girl with rather too sharp a tongue at times; she had her future nicely mapped out, and no doubt, in due course, she would make a success of her profession.

He doubted if she would marry, for she made no attempt to make herself attractive; her clothes were good, but dowdy, and her hairstyle by no means flattering. She had pretty hair too, he remembered, and there was a great deal of it. Sitting there last night in her cotton nightie she had been Mintie, and not Miss Pomfrey, but she wouldn't thank him for reminding her of that.

The boys took his attention again and he forget her.

The boys in bed, Araminta went to her room and got into the blue crêpe. A nicely judged ten minutes before dinner would be served, she went downstairs. She could see Bas putting the finishing touches to the table through the half-open dining room door as she opened the door into the drawing room. The few minutes before he announced dinner could be nicely filled with a few remarks about the boys and their day…

The doctor wasn't alone. The woman sitting opposite him was beautiful—quite the most beautiful Araminta had ever seen; she had golden hair, a straight nose, a curving mouth and large eyes. Araminta had no doubt that they were blue. She was wearing a silk trouser suit—black—and gold jewellery, and she was laughing at something the doctor had said.

Araminta took a step backwards. 'So sorry, I didn't know that you had a guest…'

The doctor got to his feet. 'Ah, Miss Pomfrey, don't go. Come and meet Mevrouw Lutyns.' And, as she crossed the room, 'Christina, this is Miss Pomfrey, who is in charge of the boys while Lucy and Jack are away.'

Mevrouw Lutyns smiled charmingly, shook hands and Araminta felt her regarding her with cold blue eyes. 'Ah, yes, the nanny. I hope you will find Utrecht interesting during your short stay here.'

Her English was almost perfect, but then she herself was almost perfect, reflected Araminta, at least to look at.

'I'm sure I shall, *Mevrouw*.' She looked at the doctor, gave a little nod and the smallest of smiles and went to the door.

'Don't go, Miss Pomfrey, you must have a drink... I shall be out this evening, by the way, but I'll leave you in Bas's good hands.'

'I came down to tell you that the boys were in bed, Doctor. I'll not stay for a drink, thank you.' She wished them good evening and a pleasant time, seething quietly.

She closed the door equally quietly, but not before she heard Mevrouw Lutyns' voice, pitched in a penetrating whisper. 'What a little dowd, Marcus. Wherever did you find her?'

She stood in the hall, trembling with rage. It was a pity she didn't understand the doctor's reply.

'That is an unkind remark, Christina. Miss Pomfrey is a charming girl and the boys are devoted to her already. Her appearance is of no consequence; I find her invaluable.'

They were speaking Dutch now, and Mevrouw Lutyns said prettily, 'Oh, my dear, I had no intention of being unkind. I'm sure she's a treasure.'

They left the house presently and dined at one of Utrecht's fine restaurants, and from time to time, much against his intention, the doctor found himself thinking about Araminta, eating her solitary dinner in the blue dress which he realised she had put on expecting to dine with him.

He drove his companion back later that evening, to her flat in one of the modern blocks away from the centre of the city. He refused her offer of a drink with the excuse that he had to go to the hospital to check on a patient, and, when she suggested that they might spend another evening together, told her that he had a number of other consultations, not only in Utrecht, and he didn't expect to be free.

An answer which didn't please her at all.

It was almost midnight as he let himself into his house. It was very quiet in the dimly lit hall but Humphrey was there, patiently waiting for his evening walk, and the doctor went out again, to walk briskly through the quiet streets with his dog. It was a fine night, but chilly, and when they got back home he took Humphrey to the kitchen, settled him in his basket and poured himself a mug of coffee from the pot keeping hot on the Aga. Presently he took himself off to bed.

The evening, he reflected, had been a waste of time. He had known Christina for some years but had thought of her as an amusing and intelligent friend; to fall in love with her had never entered his head. He supposed, as he had done from time to time, that he *would* marry, but neither she nor the other women of his acquaintance succeeded in capturing his affection. His work meant a great deal to him, and he was wealthy, and served by people he trusted and regarded as friends. He sometimes wondered if he would ever meet a woman he would love to the exclusion of everything else.

He was already at breakfast when Araminta and the two boys joined him the next day. Peter and Paul rushed to him, both talking at once, intent on reminding him that he had promised to take them out for the day at the weekend. He assured them that he hadn't forgotten and wished Araminta good morning in a friendly voice, hoping that she had forgotten the awkwardness of the previous evening.

She replied with her usual composure, settled the boys to their breakfast and poured herself a cup of coffee. She had spent a good deal of the night reminding herself that she was the boys' nanny, just as the hateful Mevrouw Lutyns had said. It had been silly to suppose that he would wish to spend what little spare time he had with her when he had friends of his own.

Probably he was in love with the woman, and Araminta couldn't blame him for that for she was so exactly right for him—all that golden hair and a lovely face, not to mention the clothes. If Mevrouw Lutyns had considered her a dowd in the blue crêpe, what on earth would she think of her in her sensible blouse and skirt? But the doctor wouldn't think of Araminta; he barely glanced at her and she didn't blame him for that.

She replied now to his civil remark about the weather and buttered a roll. She really must remember her place; she wasn't in Hambledon now, the daughter of highly respected parents, famous for their obscure Celtic learning…

The doctor took off his spectacles and looked at her. There was no sign of pique or hurt feelings, he was relieved to observe. He said pleasantly, 'I shall be taking the boys to Leiden for the day tomorrow. I'm sure you will be glad to have a day to yourself in which to explore. I have a ground map of Utrecht somewhere; I'll let you have it. There is a great deal to see and there are some good shops.'

When she thanked him, he added, 'If you should wish to stay out in the evening, Bas will let you have a key.'

She thanked him again and wondered if that was a polite hint not to return to the house until bedtime.

'What about the boys? Putting them to bed…?'

He said casually, 'Oh, Jet will see to that,' then added, 'I shall be away for most of Sunday, but I'm sure you can cope.'

'Yes, of course. I'm sure the boys will think up something exciting to do.'

The days were falling into a pattern, she reflected: school in the morning, long walks in the afternoon, shopping expeditions for postcards, books or another puzzle, and an hour to herself in the evening when the boys were with their uncle.

She no longer expected the doctor to dine with her in the evening.

All the same, for pride's sake, she got into the blue

crêpe and ate her dinner that evening with every appearance of enjoyment. She was living in the lap of comfort, she reminded herself, going back to the drawing room to sit and read the English papers Bas had thoughtfully provided for her until she could go to bed once the long case clock in the hall chimed ten o'clock.

She took a long time getting ready for bed, refusing to admit how lonely she was. Later she heard quiet footsteps in the hall and a door close. The doctor was home.

The doctor and the boys left soon after breakfast on Saturday. Araminta, standing in the hall to bid them goodbye, was hugged fiercely by Peter and Paul.

'You will be here when we get back?' asked Peter.

'Couldn't you come with us now?' Paul added urgently, and turned to his uncle, waiting patiently to usher them into the car. 'You'd like her to come, wouldn't you, Uncle?'

'Miss Pomfrey—' at a look from Peter he changed it. 'Mintie is only here for a few weeks and she wants to see as much of Utrecht as possible. This is the first chance she's had to go exploring and shopping. Women like to look at shops, you know.'

'I'll have a good look round,' promised Araminta, 'and when we go out tomorrow perhaps you can show me some of the places I won't have seen.'

She bent to kiss them and waited at the door as they got into the car, with Humphrey stretched out between them. She didn't look at the doctor.

Bas shut the door as soon as the car had gone. 'You will be in to lunch, miss?' he wanted to know. 'At any time to suit you.'

'Thank you, Bas, but I think I'll get something while I'm out; there's such a lot to see. Are you sure Jet can manage with the boys at bedtime?'

'Oh, yes, miss. The doctor has arranged that he will be out this evening...' He paused and looked awkward.

'So she won't need to cook dinner—just something for the boys.'

He looked relieved. 'I was given to understand that you would be out this evening, miss. I am to give you a key, although I will, of course, remain up until you are back.'

'How kind of you, Bas. I'll take a key, of course, but I expect I shall be back by ten o'clock. When I come in I'll leave the key on the hall table, shall I? Then you'll know that I'm in the house.'

'Thank you, miss. You will have coffee before you go out?'

'Please, Bas, if it's not too much trouble.'

She left the house a little later and began a conscientious exploration of the city. The boys would want to know what she had seen and where she had been... She had been to the Domkerk with them, now she went to the Dom Tower and then through the cloister passage to the University Chapter Hall. The Central Museum was next on her list—costumes, jewellery, some paintings and beautiful furniture. By now it was well after noon, so she looked for a small café and lingered over a *kaas broodje*. She would have liked more but she had no idea when she would be paid and she hadn't a great deal of money.

The day, which had begun with sunshine and gentle wind, had become overcast, and the wind was no longer gentle. She was glad of her jacket over the jersey two-piece as she made her way to the shopping centre. The shops were fine, filled with beautiful things: clothes, of course, and shoes, but as well as these splendid furniture, porcelain, silver and glass… There were bookshops, too, and she spent a long time wandering round them, wishing she could buy some of their contents. It surprised her to find so many English books on sale, and to find a shop selling Burberrys and Harris Tweed. It would be no hardship to live here, she reflected, and took herself off to find the *hofjes* and patrician houses, to stand and admire their age-old beauty.

She found another small coffee shop where she had tea and a cake while she pondered what to do with her evening. She thought she might go back around nine o'clock. By then the boys would be in bed and asleep, and if the doctor was out, Bas and Jet would be in kitchen. A cinema seemed the answer. It would mean that she couldn't afford a meal, but she could buy a sandwich and a cup of coffee before she went back to the house.

There were several cinemas; she chose one in a square in the centre of the city, paid out most of her remaining guldens and sat through an American film. Since she was a little tired by now, she dozed off and woke to see that it was over and that the advertisements were on. After that the lights went up and everyone went out into the street.

It was almost dark now, but it was still barely eight o'clock. She went into a crowded café and had a cup of coffee, then decided that she had better save what guldens she had left. There was a small tin of biscuits by her bed; she could eat those. She couldn't sit for ever over one cup of coffee, though, so she went into the street and started her walk back to the house.

She was crossing the square when she saw the little stall at one corner. *Pommes Frites* was painted across its wooden front.

'Chips,' said Araminta, her mouth watering. 'But why do they have to say so in French when we're in Holland?' She went over to the corner and in exchange for two gulden was handed a little paper cornet filled with crisp golden chips. She bit into one; it was warm and crunchy and delicious...

Dr van der Breugh, on his way to dine with old friends, halting at traffic lights, glanced around him. Being a Saturday evening there were plenty of people about; the cafés and restaurants were doing a good trade and the various stalls had plenty of customers.

He saw Araminta as the light changed, and he had to drive on, but instead of going straight ahead, as he should have done, he turned back towards the square and stopped the car a few feet from her.

She hadn't seen him; he watched her bite into a chip with the eager delight of a child and then choke on it when she looked up and saw him. He was astonished at his feelings of outrage at the sight of her. Outrage at his own behaviour. He should have taken her with them, or at least made some arrangement for her day. He got out of his car, his calm face showing nothing of his feelings.

As for Araminta, if the ground had obligingly opened and allowed her to fall into it, she would have been happy; as it was, she would have to do the best she could. She swallowed the last fragment of chip and said politely, 'Good evening, doctor. What delicious chips you have in Holland...'

He had no intention of wasting time talking about chips. 'Why are you here, Miss Pomfrey? Why are you not at the house, eating your dinner....' He paused, frowning. He hadn't given her a thought when he returned with the boys, hadn't asked Bas if she was back, had forgotten her.

Araminta saw the frown and made haste to explain. 'Well, you see, it's like this. Bas thought that I would be out until late; he gave me a key, too, so I expect there was a misunderstanding. I thought—' she caught his eye '—well, I thought that perhaps you expected me to stay out. I mean, you did say that Jet would put the boys to bed, so you didn't expect me back, did you?' She hesitated. 'Am I making myself clear?'

When he didn't speak, she added, 'I've had a most

interesting day, and I went to the cinema this evening. I'm on my way back to the house now, so I'll say good evening, doctor.'

'No, Miss Pomfrey, you will not say good evening. You will come with me and we will have dinner together. I have no doubt that you have eaten nothing much all day and I cannot forgive myself for not seeing that you had adequate money with you and arrangements made for your free day. Please forgive me?'

She stared up at him, towering over her. 'Of course I forgive you. I'm not your guest, you know, and I'm quite used to being by myself. And please don't feel that you have to give me a meal; I've just eaten all those chips.'

'All the same, we will dine together.' He swept her into the car and picked up the car phone. He spoke in Dutch so that she wasn't to know that he was excusing himself from a dinner party.

'Oh, that hospital again,' said his hostess. 'Do you never get a free moment, Marcus?'

He made a laughing rejoinder, promised to dine at some future date, and started the car.

Araminta, still clutching her chips, said in a tight little voice, 'Will you take me back to the house, doctor? It's kind of you to offer me a meal, but I'm not hungry.'

A waste of breath, for all she got in reply was a grunt as he swept the car back into the lighted streets, past shop windows still blazing with light, cafés spilling out onto the pavements, grand hotels... She tried again. 'I'm not suitably dressed...'

He took no notice of that either, but turned into a narrow side street lined with elegant little shops. At its far end there was a small restaurant.

There was a canal on the opposite side of the street, and the doctor parked beside it—dangerously near the edge, from her point of view—and got out. There was no help for it but to get out when he opened her door, to be marched across the street and into the restaurant.

It was a small place: a long, narrow room with tables well apart, most of them occupied. Araminta was relieved to see that although the women there were well dressed, several of them were in suits and dark dresses so that her jacket and skirt weren't too conspicuous.

It seemed the doctor was known there; they were led to a table in one corner, her jacket was taken from her and a smiling waiter drew out her chair.

The doctor sat down opposite to her. 'What will you drink?' he asked. 'Dry sherry?'

When she agreed, he spoke to the waiter, who offered menus. There was choice enough, and she saw at a glance that everything was wildly expensive. She stared down at it; she hadn't wanted to come, and it would be entirely his fault if she chose caviar, plover's eggs and truffles, all of which were on the menu, their cost equivalent to a week's housekeeping money. On the other hand, she had no wish to sample any of these delicacies and, since she must have spoilt his evening, it seemed only fair to choose as economically as possible.

The doctor put down his menu. 'Unless you would like anything special, will you leave it to me to order?'

'Oh, please.' She added, 'There's such a lot to choose from, isn't there?'

'Indeed. How about marinated aubergine to start with? And would you like sea bass to follow?'

She agreed; she wasn't shy, and she was too much her parents' daughter to feel awkward. She had never been in a restaurant such as this one, but she wasn't going to let it intimidate her. When the food came she ate with pleasure and, mindful of manners, made polite conversation. The doctor was at first secretly amused and then found himself interested. Miss Pomfrey might be nothing out of the ordinary, but she had self-assurance and a way of looking him in the eye which he found disquieting. Not a conceited man, but aware of his worth, he wasn't used to being studied in such a manner.

For a moment he regretted his spoilt evening, but told himself that he was being unjust and then suggested that she might like a pudding from the trolley.

She chose sticky toffee pudding and ate it with enjoyment, and he, watching her over his biscuits and cheese, found himself reluctantly liking her.

They had talked in a guarded fashion over their meal—the weather, the boys, her opinion of Utrecht, all safe subjects. It was when they got back to the house and she had thanked him and started for the stairs that he stopped her.

'Miss Pomfrey, we do not need to refer again to the regrettable waste of your free day. Rest assured that I shall see to it that any other free time you have will be well spent.'

'Thank you, but I am quite capable of looking after myself.'

He smiled thinly. 'Allow me to be the best judge of that, Miss Pomfrey.' He turned away. 'Goodnight.'

She paused on the stairs. 'Goodnight, doctor.' And then she added, 'I bought the chips because I was hungry. I dare say you would have done the same,' she told him in a matter-of-fact voice.

The doctor watched her small retreating back and went into his study. Presently he began to laugh.

CHAPTER FOUR

ARAMINTA woke early on Sunday morning and remembered that the doctor had said that he would be away all day—moreover, he had remarked that he had no doubt that she and the boys would enjoy their day. Doing what? she wondered, and sat up and worried about it until Jet came in with her morning tea, a concession to her English habit.

They smiled and nodded at each other and exchanged a *'Goeden Morgen'*, and the boys, hearing Jet's voice, came into the room and got onto Araminta's bed to eat the little biscuits which had come with the tea.

'We have to get up and dress,' they told her. 'We go to church with Uncle Marcus at half past nine.'

'Oh, do you? Then back to your room, boys, I'll be along in ten minutes or so.'

Church would last about an hour, she supposed, which meant that a good deal of the morning would be gone; they could go to one of the parks and feed the ducks, then come back for lunch, and by then surely she would have thought of something to fill the afternoon hours. A pity it wasn't raining, then they could have stayed indoors.

Jet had told her that breakfast would be at half past

eight—at least, Araminta was almost sure that was what she had said; she knew the word for breakfast by now, and the time of day wasn't too hard to guess at. She dressed and went to help the boys. Not that they needed much help, for they dressed themselves, even if a bit haphazardly. But she brushed hair, tied miniature ties and made sure that their teeth were brushed and their hands clean. She did it without fuss; at the children's convalescent home there had been no time to linger over such tasks.

The doctor wasn't at breakfast, and they had almost finished when he came in with Humphrey. He had been for a walk, he told them. Humphrey had needed to stretch his legs. He sat down and had a cup of coffee, explaining that he had already breakfasted. 'Church at half past nine,' he reminded them, and asked Araminta if she would care to go with them. 'The church is close by—a short walk—you might find it interesting.'

She sensed that he expected her to accept. 'Thank you, I would like to come,' she told him. 'At what time are we to be ready?'

'Ten past nine. The service lasts about an hour.'

They each had a child's hand as they walked to the church, which was small and old, smelling of damp, flowers and age and, to Araminta's mind, rather bleak. They sat right at the front in a high-backed pew with narrow seats and hassocks. The boys sat between them, standing on the hassocks to sing the hymns and then sitting through a lengthy sermon.

Of course, Araminta understood very little of the service, although some of the hymn tunes were the same, but the sermon, preached by an elderly dominee with a flowing beard, sounded as though it was threatening them with severe punishments in the hereafter; she was relieved when it ended with a splendid rolling period of unintelligible words and they all sang a hymn.

It was a tune she knew, but the words in the hymn book the doctor had thoughtfully provided her with were beyond her understanding. The boys sang lustily, as did the doctor, in a deep rumbling voice, and since they were singing so loudly, she hummed the tune to herself. It was the next best thing.

Back at the house, the doctor asked Bas to bring coffee into the drawing room.

'I shall be leaving in a few minutes,' he told Araminta. 'I expect you intend to take a walk before lunch, but in the afternoon Bas will drive you to Steijner's toy shop. They have an exhibition of toys there today and I have tickets. And next door there is a café where you may have your tea. Bas will come for you at about five o'clock. If you want him earlier, telephone the house.'

The boys were delighted, and so was Araminta, although she didn't allow it to show. The day had been nicely taken care of and the boys were going to enjoy themselves. She had no doubt that she would too.

The doctor stooped to kiss the boys. 'Have fun,' he

told them, and to Araminta, 'Enjoy your afternoon, Miss Pomfrey. I leave the boys in your safe hands.'

It was only after he had gone that she realised that she hadn't much money—perhaps not enough to pay for their tea. She need not have worried. The boys showed her the notes their uncle had given to them to spend and a moment later, Bas, coming to collect the coffee cups, told her quietly that there was an envelope for her in the doctor's study if she would be good enough to fetch it.

There was, in her opinion, enough money in it to float a ship. She counted it carefully, determined to account for every cent of it, and went back to collect the boys ready for their walk.

They decided against going to one of the parks but instead they walked to one of the squares, the *'neude'*, and so into the Oudegracht, where there was the four-teenth-century house in which the Treaty of Utrecht had been signed. They admired the patrician house at some length, until Araminta said, 'Are we very far from your uncle's house? We should be getting back.'

They chorused reassurance. 'Look, Mintie, we just go back to the *neude* and Vredeburg Square, and it's only a little way then.'

She had been there the day before, spending hours looking at the windows of the shopping centre. The doctor's house was only a short distance from the Singel, the moat which surrounded the old city— much of its length was lined with attractive prome-nades backed by impressive houses.

'By the time we go home I shall know quite a lot about Utrecht,' she told the boys. 'Now, let's go back to the house and have lunch; we don't want to miss one moment of the exhibition…'

Steijner's toy shop was vast, housed in a narrow building, several storeys high, each floor reached by a narrow, steep staircase. The front shop was large and opened out into another smaller room which extended, long and narrow, as far as a blank wall. Both rooms were lined with shelves packed with toys of every description, and arranged down their centres were the larger exhibits: miniature motor cars, dolls' houses, minute bicycles, magnificent model boats.

The place was crowded with children, tugging the grown-ups to and fro, and it was some time before Araminta and the boys managed to climb the first flight of stairs to the floor above. The rooms here were mostly given over to dolls, more dolls' houses and miniature kitchens and furniture, so they stayed only for a few minutes and then, together with a great many other people, made their way to the next floor.

This was very much more to the boy's liking—more cars and bikes, kites of every kind, skates, trumpets and drums, puppets and toy animals. Araminta, with the beginnings of a headache, suggested hopefully that they might go and have their tea and wait for Bas in the café. More and more people were filling the shop, the narrow stairs were packed, but the children were reluctant to move from the displays they fancied.

'There's camping stuff on the next floor,' said Peter, and he tugged at her hand. 'Could we just have a look—a quick peep?' He looked so appealing and since Paul had joined him, raising an excited face to her, she gave in. 'All right. But we won't stay too long, mind.'

The last flight of stairs was very narrow and steep, and the room it led to was low-ceilinged and narrow, with a slit window set in the gable. But it was well lit and the array of camping equipment was impressive. There were only a handful of people there and before long they had gone back down the staircase, leaving the boys alone to examine the tents and camping equipment to their hearts' content.

They must have a tent, they told Araminta excitedly, they would ask Uncle Marcus to buy them one. 'We could live in it in the garden, Mintie. You'd come too, of course.'

They went round and round, trying to decide which tent was the one they liked best. They were still longing to have one and arguing about it when Araminta looked at her watch.

'Time for tea, my dears,' she told them. 'We mustn't keep Bas waiting.'

It was another five minutes before she could prise them away and start down the stairs in single file. Peter was in front and he stopped on the last stair.

'The door's shut,' he said.

Araminta reached over. 'Well, we'll just turn the handle.'

Only there wasn't a handle, only an old-fashioned lock with no key. She changed places with Peter and gave the door a good push. Nothing happened; the door could have been rock. She told the boys to sit on the stairs and knocked hard. There was no reply, nor did anyone answer her 'hello'. The place was quiet, though when she looked at her watch she wondered why. The exhibition was due to close at five o'clock and it was fifteen minutes to that hour. All the same, surely someone would tour the building and make sure that everyone had left. She shouted, uneasily aware of the thickness of the door.

'What an adventure!' she said bracingly. 'Let's all shout…'

Which brought no result whatever.

'Well, we'd better go back to the room. Someone will come presently; it's not quite time for people to have to leave yet.' She spoke in a matter-of-fact voice and hoped that the boys would believe her.

Back upstairs again, she went to the narrow window. The glass was thick and, although it had once opened, it had been long since sealed up. She looked around for something suitable to break it, picked up a tent peg and, urged on by the boys, who were revelling in the whole thing, began to bash the glass.

It didn't break easily, and only some of it fell into the street below, but anyone passing or standing nearby could have seen it. She shouted hopefully, unaware that there was no one there. The doctor's sec-

ond car, another Jaguar, was standing close by, but
Bas had gone into the café to see if they were there.

Of course, they weren't; he went to the toy shop,
where the doors were being locked.

'Everyone has left,' he was told, and when he
asked why they had closed a quarter of an hour sooner
than expected, he was told that an electrical fault had
been found and it was necessary to turn off the cur-
rent.

'But no one's inside,' he was assured by the owner,
who was unaware that the assistant who had checked
the place hadn't bothered to go to the top room but
had locked the door and gone home.

They could have gone back to the house, thought
Bas. Miss Pomfrey was a sensible young woman, and
instead of lingering about waiting for him she would
have taken the boys home to let him know that they
had left earlier than they had planned.

He got into the car and drove back, to find the
Bentley parked by the canal and the doctor in his
study. He looked up as Bas went in, but before he
could speak Bas said urgently, 'You're just this minute back, *mijnheer*? You do not know about the exhibition closing early? I thought Miss Pomfrey and
the boys would be here.'

The doctor was out of his chair. 'At the toy shop?
It is closed? Why? You're sure? They were not in the
café?'

'No one had seen them. I spoke to the man closing
the place—there's been an electrical fault, that's why

they shut early. He was sure that there was no one left inside.'

The doctor was already at the door. 'They can't be far, and Miss Pomfrey isn't a girl to lose her head. Come along. We'll find them. You stay in the car, Bas, in case they turn up.'

With Bas beside him he drove to Steijner's shop. There were few people about—the proprietor and his assistants had gone home—but there was a van parked outside and men unloading equipment.

The doctor parked the car and walked over to them. 'You have keys? I believe there are two boys and a young woman still inside. I'm not sure of it, but I must check.'

He looked up as a small splattering of glass fell between them. He looked up again and saw what appeared to be a stocking waving from the gabled window.

The man looked up, too. 'Best get them down, *mijnheer*. I'll open up—you won't need help? I've quite a bit of work here...'

He opened the door, taking his time over its bolts and chains, giving the doctor time to allow for his relief, mingled, for some reason which he didn't understand, with rising rage. The silly girl. Why didn't she leave the place with everyone else? There must have been some other people there, and the boys would have understood what was said—everyone would have been warned in good time.

He raced up the stairs, turned the key in the lock

of the last door and went up the staircase two at a
time. The boys rushed to meet him, bubbling about
their adventure, delighted to see him, and he put his
great arms around their small shoulders.

He said, very softly, 'I hope you have a good ex-
planation for this, Miss Pomfrey.' The look he gave
her shrivelled her bones.

Araminta, ready and eager to explain, bit back the
words. He was furiously angry with her. No doubt
any other man would have sworn at her and called
her names, but he had spoken with an icy civility
which sent shivers down her spine. A pity he hadn't
shouted, she reflected, then she could have shouted
back. Instead she said nothing at all, and after a moment he turned to the boys.

'Bas is below with the car. If you haven't had tea
we will have it together.'

'Shall we tell you about it, Uncle Marcus?' began
Peter.

'Later, Peter, after tea.' He crossed the room and
took Araminta's stocking off the glass window. It was
hopelessly torn and laddered, but he handed it to her
very politely. Her 'thank you' was equally polite, but
she didn't look at him. She felt a fool with only one
stocking, and he had contrived to make her feel guilty
about something which hadn't been her fault. Nor had
he asked what had happened, but had condemned her
unheard.

At the bottom of the staircase she paused; she
would show him that there was no handle on the door.

But he was already going down the next stairs with the boys.

She was going to call him back, but his impatient, 'Come along, Miss Pomfrey,' gave her no chance. She followed the three of them out to the car and got in wordlessly. Once back at the house, she tidied up the boys ready for tea, excused herself on account of a headache and went to her room.

The doctor's curled lip at her excuse boded ill for any further conversation he might wish to have with her. And she had no doubt that he would have more to say about feather-brained women who got left behind and locked up while in charge of small boys....

Bas brought in the tea. 'Miss Pomfrey will be with you presently?' he wanted to know. He had seen her pale face and his master's inscrutable features in the car. 'You could have cut the air between them with a pair of scissors,' he had told Jet.

'Miss Pomfrey has a headache. Perhaps you would take her a tray of tea,' suggested the doctor.

'Mintie never has a headache,' declared Peter. 'She said so; she said she's never ill...'

'In that case, I dare say she will be with us again in a short time,' observed his uncle. 'I see that Jet has baked a *boterkoek*, and there are *krentenbollejes*...'

'Currant buns,' said Paul. 'Shall we save one for Mintie?'

'Why not? Now, tell me, did you enjoy the exhibition? Was there anything that you both liked?'

'A tent—that's why we were in the room at the

very top. It was full of tents and things for camping. We though we'd like a tent. Mintie said she'd come and live in it with us in the garden. She made us laugh, 'specially when we tried to open the door...'

The doctor put down his tea cup. 'And it wouldn't open?'

'It was a real adventure. Mintie supposed that the people who went downstairs before us forgot and shut the door, and of course there wasn't a handle. You would have enjoyed it, too, Uncle. We banged on the door and shouted, and then Mintie broke the glass in the window and took off a stocking and hung it through the hole she'd made. She said it was what those five children in the Enid Blyton books would have done and we were having an adventure. It was real fun, wasn't it, Peter?'

His uncle said, 'It sounds a splendid adventure.'

'I 'spect that's why Mintie's got a headache,' said Peter.

'I believe you may be right, Peter. Have we finished tea? Would you both like to take Humphrey into the garden? He likes company. I have something to do, so if I'm not here presently, go to Jet in the kitchen, will you?'

The boys ran off, shouting and laughing, throwing a ball for the good-natured Humphrey, and when Bas came to clear away the tea things, the doctor said, 'Bas, would you be good enough to ask Miss Pomfrey to come to my study as soon as she feels better?'

He crossed the hall and shut the study door behind

him, and Bas went back to the kitchen. Jet, told of this, pooh-poohed the idea that the doctor was about to send Miss Pomfrey packing. 'More like he's got the wrong end of the stick about what happened this afternoon and wants to know what did happen. You don't know?'

Bas shook his head. 'No idea. But it wasn't anything to upset the boys; they were full of their adventure.'

Araminta had drunk her tea, had a good cry, washed her face and applied powder and lipstick once more, tidied her hair and sat down to think. She had no intention of telling the doctor anything; he was arrogant, ill-tempered and she couldn't bear the sight of him. Anyone else would have asked her what had happened, given her a chance to explain. He had taken it for granted that she had been careless and unreliable. 'I hate him,' said Araminta, not meaning it, but it relieved her feelings.

When Bas came for the tea tray and gave her the message from the doctor she thanked him and said that she would be down presently. When he had gone she went to the gilt edged triple mirror on the dressing table and took a good look. Viewed from all sides, her face looked much as usual. Slightly puffy eyelids could be due to the headache. Perhaps another light dusting of powder on her nose, which was still pink at its tip... She practised one or two calm and dignified expressions and rehearsed several likely an-

swers to the cross questioning she expected, and, thus
fortified, went down to the study.

The doctor was sitting at his desk, but he got up
as she went in.

He said at once, 'Please sit down, Miss Pomfrey, I
owe you an apology. It was unpardonable of me to
speak to you in such a fashion, to give you no chance
to explain—'

Araminta chipped in, 'It's quite all right, doctor, I
quite understand. You must have been very worried.'

'Were you not worried, Mintie?'

He so seldom called her that that she stared at him.
His face was as impassive as it always was; he was
looking at her over his spectacles, his brows lifted in
enquiry.

'Me? Yes, of course I was. I was scared out of my
wits, if you must know—so afraid that the boys would
suddenly realise that we might be shut up for hours
and it wasn't an adventure, after all.' She added matter-of-factly, 'Of course, I knew you'd come sooner
or later.'

'Oh, and why should you be so sure of that?'

She frowned. 'I don't know—at least, I suppose…
I don't know.'

'I hope you accept my apology, and if there is anything—'

'Of course I accept it,' she interrupted him again.
'And there isn't anything. Thank you.'

'You are happy here? You do not find it too dull?'

'I don't see how anyone could feel dull with Peter and Paul as companions.'

She looked at him and smiled.

'You have been crying, Miss Pomfrey?'

So she was Miss Pomfrey again. 'Certainly not. What have I got to cry about?'

'I can think of several things, and you may be a splendid governess, Miss Pomfrey, but you are a poor liar.'

She went rather red in the face. 'What a nasty thing to say about me,' she snapped, quite forgetting that he was her employer, who expected politeness at all times, no doubt, 'I never tell lies, not the kind which harm people. Besides, my father has always told me that a weeping woman is a thorn in the flesh of any man.'

The doctor kept a straight face. 'A very sensible opinion,' he murmured. 'All the same, if it was I who caused your tears, I'm sorry. I have no wish to upset you or make you unhappy.'

She sought for an answer, but since she couldn't think of one, she stayed silent.

'You behaved with commendable good sense.' He smiled then. 'Dr Jenkell assured me that you were the most level-headed young woman he had ever known. I must be sure and tell him how right he was.'

If that's a compliment, thought Araminta, I'd as soon do without it. She wondered what would have happened if she had been pretty and empty-headed and screamed her head off. Men being men, they would have rushed to her rescue, poured brandy down her throat and offered a shoulder for her to cry into. They would probably have called her poor little girl and made sure that she went to her bed for the rest of the day. And the doctor was very much a man, wasn't he? Being plain had its drawbacks, thought Araminta.

The doctor, watching her expressive face, wondered what she was thinking. How fortunate it was that she was such a sensible girl. The whole episode would be forgotten, but he must remember to make sure that her next free day was a success.

He said now, 'I expect you want to go to the boys. I told them that they might have supper with us this evening, but that they must have their baths and be ready for bed first.'

Dismissed, but with her evening's work already planned, Araminta went in search of the boys and spent the next hour supervising the cleaning of teeth, the brushing of hair and the riotous bath. With the boys looking like two small angels, she led them downstairs presently. There had been little time to do anything to her own person; she had dabbed her nose with powder, brushed her own hair, and sighed into the mirror, aware that the doctor wouldn't notice if she wore a blonde wig and false eyelashes.

'Not that I mind in the least,' she had told her reflection.

Her supposition was regrettably true, he barely glanced at her throughout the meal, and when he did he didn't see anyone other than the dependable Miss Pomfrey, suitably merging into the background of his life.

The next days were uneventful, a pleasant pattern of mornings at school, afternoons spent exploring and evenings playing some game or other. When their uncle was at home, the boys spent their short evenings with him, leaving her free to do whatever she wanted.

She supposed that she could have gone and sat in the little room behind the drawing room and watched the TV, but no one had suggested it and she didn't like to go there uninvited. So she stayed in her room, doing her nails, sewing on buttons and mending holes in small garments. It was a pleasant room, warm and nicely furnished, but it didn't stop her feeling lonely.

It was towards the end of the week that Paul got up one morning and didn't want his breakfast. Probably a cold, thought Araminta, and kept an eye on him.

He seemed quite his usual self when she fetched them both from school, but by the evening he was feverish, peevish and thoroughly out of sorts. It was a pity that the doctor had gone to the Hague and wouldn't be back until late that evening. Araminta put him to bed and, since the twins didn't like to be separated, Peter had his bath and got ready for bed, too. With Bas's help she carried up their light supper.

But Paul didn't want his; his throat was sore and his head ached and when she took his temperature it was alarmingly high. She sat him on her lap, persuaded him to drink the cold drinks Bas brought and, while Peter finished his supper, embarked on a story. She made it up as she went along, and it was about nothing in particular, but the boys listened and presently Paul went to sleep, his hot little head pressed against her shoulder.

Peter had come to sit beside her, and she put an arm around him, carrying on a cheerful whispered conversation until he, reassured about his brother, slept too.

It was some time later when Bas came in quietly to remind her that dinner was waiting for her.

'I'm sorry, Bas, but I can't come. They're both sound asleep and Paul isn't well. They're bound to wake presently, then I can put them in their beds... Will you apologize to Jet for me? I'm not hungry; I can have some soup later.'

Bas went reluctantly and she was left, her insides rumbling, while she tried not to think of food. Just like the doctor, she thought testily, to be away just when he was wanted. She wouldn't allow herself to panic. She had coped with childish ailments at the children's convalescent home and knew how resilient they were and how quickly they got well once whatever it was which had afflicted them had been diagnosed and dealt with. All the same, she wished that the doctor would come home soon.

Minutes ticked themselves slowly into an hour, but she managed a cheerful smile when Bas put a concerned head round the door.

'They'll wake soon,' she assured him in a whisper. But they slept on: Peter sleeping the deep sleep of a healthy child, Paul deeply asleep too but with a mounting fever, his tousled head still against her shoulder. She longed to changed her position; she longed even more for a cup of tea. It did no good to dwell on that, so she allowed her thoughts free rein and wondered what the doctor was doing and who he was with. She hoped that whoever it was wasn't distracting him from returning home at a reasonable hour.

It was a good thing that she didn't know that on the point of his leaving the hospital in the Hague he had been urgently recalled...

When he did get home it was ten o'clock. Bas came hurrying into the hall to meet him, his nice elderly face worried.

'What's wrong?' asked the doctor.

'Little Paul. He's not well, *mijnheer*. He's asleep, but Miss Pomfrey has him on her lap; he's been there for hours. Peter's there too. Miss Pomfrey asked me to phone the hospital, but you were not available...'

The doctor put a hand on Bas's shoulder. 'I'll go up. Don't worry, Bas.'

Araminta had heard him come home, and the voices in the hall, and relief flooded through her. She peered down into Paul's sleeping face and then looked up as the doctor came quietly into the room.

'Have you had the mumps?' she asked him.

He stopped short. 'Good Lord, yes, decades ago.'

He looked at his nephew's face, showing distinct signs of puffiness, then stopped and lifted him gently off her lap.

'How long have you been sitting there?'

'Since six o'clock. He's got a temperature and a headache and his throat's sore. Peter's all right so far.'

The doctor laid the still sleeping boy in his bed and bent to examine him gently. 'We will let him sleep, poor scrap.' He came and took Peter in his arms and tucked him up in his bed, talking softly to the half-awake child. Only then did he turn to Araminta, sitting, perforce, exactly as she had been doing for the past few hours, so stiff that she didn't dare to move.

The doctor hauled her gently to her feet, put an arm around her and walked her up and down.

'Now, go downstairs, tell Bas to ask Jet to get us something to eat and send Nel up here to sit with the boys for a while.'

And when she hesitated, he added, 'Go along, Miss Pomfrey. I want my supper.'

She gave him a speaking look; she wanted her supper, too, and the unfeeling man hadn't even bothered to ask her if she needed hers.

'So do I,' she snapped, and then added, 'Is Paul all right? It is only mumps?'

He said coolly, 'Yes, Miss Pomfrey. Hopefully only mumps.'

She went downstairs and gave Bas his messages, then went and sat in the small sitting room. She was tired and rather untidy and she could see ahead of her several trying days while the mumps kept their hold on Paul—and possibly Peter.

'Twelve days incubation,' she said, talking to herself, 'and we could wait longer than that until we're sure Peter doesn't get them, too.'

'Inevitable, Miss Pomfrey. Do you often talk to yourself?'

The doctor had come silently into the room. He poured a glass of sherry and gave it to her and didn't wait for her answer. 'It will mean bed for a few days for Paul, and of course Peter can't go to school. Will you be able to manage? Nel can take over in the afternoons while you take Peter for a walk?'

He watched her toss back the sherry and refilled her glass. Perhaps he was expecting too much of her. 'See how you go on,' he told her kindly. 'If necessary, I'll get some more help.'

'If Peter were to get the mumps within the next few days I shall be able to manage very nicely,' she said matter-of-factly.

'It is to be hoped that he will. Let us get them over with, by all means.'

Bas came then, so she finished her second sherry far too quickly and went to the dining room with the doctor.

Jet had conjured up an excellent meal: mushroom soup, a cheese soufflé, salad and a lemon mousse. Araminta, slightly light-headed from the sherry, ate everything put before her, making somewhat muddled conversation as she did so. The doctor watched with faint amusement as she polished off the last of the mousse.

'Now go to bed, Miss Pomfrey. You will be called as usual in the morning.'

'Oh, that won't do at all,' she told him, emboldened by the sherry. 'I'll have a bath and get ready for bed, then I'll go and sit with the boys for a bit. Once I'm sure they are all right, I'll go to bed. I shall hear them if they wake.'

'You will do as I say. I have a good deal of reading to do; I will do it in their room.'

'Aren't you going to the hospital in the morning?'

'Certainly I am.'

'Then you can't do that; you'll be like a wet rag in the morning. You need your sleep.'

'I'm quite capable of knowing how much sleep I need, Miss Pomfrey. Kindly do as I ask. Goodnight.'

She wanted to cry, although she didn't know why, but she held back the tears, wished him a bleak goodnight and went upstairs. She felt better after a hot bath, and, wrapped in her dressing gown, she crept into the boys' room to make sure they were asleep. Nel, the housemaid, had gone downstairs again and they slept peacefully. Promising herself that she would get up during the night to make sure that they were all right, Araminta took herself off to bed.

She was asleep at once, but woke instantly at a peevish wail from Paul. She tumbled out of bed and crept to the half-open door. Paul was awake and the doctor was sitting on his bed, giving him a drink.

There were papers scattered all over the floor and the chair was drawn up to the table by the window. She crept back to bed. It was two o'clock in the morning. She lay and worried about the doctor's lack of sleep until she slept once more.

She was up very early, to find the boys sleeping and the doctor gone. She dressed, crept down to the kitchen and made herself tea, filled a jug with cold lemonade and went back to the boys' room. They were still asleep. Paul's face was very swollen but Peter looked normal. She had no idea how she would manage for the next few days; it depended on whether Peter got mumps, too.

She was going silently around the room, getting clean clothes for the boys, when the doctor came in.

She wished him a quiet good morning and saw how tired he was, despite his immaculate appearance. Despite his annoyance the previous evening, she said in her sensible way, 'I hope you'll have the good sense to have a good night's sleep tonight. What would we do if you were to be ill?'

'My dear Miss Pomfrey, stop fussing. I am never ill. If you're worried during the day, tell Bas; he knows where to find me.'

And he had gone again, with a casual nod, hardly looking at her.

CHAPTER FIVE

THE day was every bit as bad as Araminta had expected it to be. Paul woke up peevish, hot and sorry for himself, and it took a good deal of coaxing to get him washed and into clean pyjamas, his temperature taken and a cold drink swallowed. Bas had produced some coloured straws, which eased the drinking problem, but the mumps had taken hold for the moment and her heart ached for the small swollen face.

Nevertheless, she got through the day, reading to the invalid until she was hoarse, playing games with Peter and then taking him for a walk with Humphrey while Nel sat with Paul. They returned, much refreshed, armed with drawing books, crayons, a jigsaw puzzle and a couple of comics, had their tea with Humphrey in the sitting room and then went to spend the rest of the afternoon with Paul. He still felt ill, but his headache was better, he said, although it still hurt him to swallow.

'You'll feel better tomorrow,' Araminta assured him. 'Not quite well, but better, and when your uncle comes home I expect he'll know what to do to take away the pain in your throat.'

The doctor came home just after six o'clock, coming into the boys' room quietly, his civil good evening to Araminta drowned in the boisterous greeting from Peter and the hoarse voice of Paul. Humphrey, who had been lying on his bed, lumbered up to add his welcome and the doctor stooped to pat him.

Before the doctor could voice any disapproval of dogs on beds, Araminta said firmly, 'I said that Humphrey could get on the bed. He's company for Paul and comforting, too, so if you want to scold anyone, please scold me.'

He looked at her with raised eyebrows and a little smile which held no warmth. 'I was not aware that I had given my opinion on the matter, Miss Pomfrey. I see no reason to scold anyone, either you or Humphrey.'

And, having disposed of the matter, he proceeded to ask her how the day had gone. He sat on the bed while she told him, examining Paul's face and neck, taking his temperature, listening to his small bony chest, looking down his throat.

'You're better,' he declared cheerfully. 'You're going to feel horrible for a few days, and you'll have to stay in bed for a while, but I've no doubt that Miss Pomfrey will keep you amused.'

'Does Miss Pomfrey—well, you mean Mintie, of course—amuse you too, Uncle?' This from Peter.

The doctor glanced across at Araminta. 'Oh, decidedly,' he said, and smiled at her, a warm smile this time, inviting her to share the joke.

It was impossible to resist that smile. She agreed cheerfully and listened to Peter, like all small boys, enlarging upon the idea with gruff chuckles from his twin.

The doctor got up presently. 'Ice cream and yoghurt for supper,' he suggested. 'Miss Pomfrey, if you would come down to my study, I will give you something to ease that sore throat. Peter, I leave you in charge for a few minutes.'

In the study, with Humphrey standing between them, he said, 'You have had a long day. I'm afraid the next few days will be equally long. Paul is picking up nicely, and the swelling should go down in another five or six days. He must stay in bed for another day or so, then he could be allowed to get up, wrapped up warmly and kept in the room. Peter seems all right…'

'Yes, and so good with his brother.'

'I shall be at home this evening. I'll keep an eye on the boys while you have dinner, and then if you would be with them for half an hour or so, I'll take over. You could do with an early night…'

She said, before she could stop her tongue, 'Do I look so awful?'

He surveyed her coolly. 'Let us say you do not look at your best, Miss Pomfrey.'

He took no notice of her glare but went to his case. 'Crush one of these and stir it into Paul's ice cream. Get him to drink as much as possible.' He added, 'You will, of course, be experienced in the treatment of childish ailments?'

'Yes,' said Araminta. The horrible man. What did

he expect when she'd been kept busy the whole day with the boys? Not look her best, indeed!

She went to the door and he opened it for her and then made matters worse by observing, 'Never mind, Miss Pomfrey, as soon as the mumps have been routed, you shall have all the time you want for beauty treatment and shopping.'

She spun round to face him, looking up into his bland face. 'Why bother? And how dare you mock me? You are an exceedingly tiresome man, but I don't suppose anyone has dared to tell you so!'

He stared down at her, not speaking.

'Oh, dear, I shouldn't have said that,' said Araminta. 'I'm sorry if I've hurt your feelings, although I don't see why I should be, for you have no regard for mine. Anyway,' she added defiantly, 'it's a free world and I can say what I like.'

'Indeed you can, Miss Pomfrey. Feel free to express your feelings whenever you have the need.'

He held the door wide and she flounced through. Back with the boys once more, she wondered if he would give her the sack. He was entitled to do so; she had been more than a little outspoken. On the other hand, he would have to get someone to replace her pretty smartly, someone willing to cope with two small boys and the mumps...

Apparently he had no such intention. Paul was soon readied for the night and Peter was prancing round in his pyjamas, demanding that he should have his supper with his brother.

'Well, I don't see why not,' said Araminta. 'Put on your dressing gown, there's a good boy, and I'll see what Bas says...'

'And what should Bas say?' asked the doctor, coming in in his usual quiet fashion.

'That he won't mind helping me bring supper up here for Peter as well as Paul.'

'By all means. Ask him to do so, Miss Pomfrey, and then have your dinner—a little early, but I dare say you will enjoy a long evening to yourself.'

There was nothing to say to that, so she went in search of Bas.

Peter said. 'You must say Mintie, Uncle. Why do you always call her Miss Pomfrey?'

'I have a shocking memory. How about a game of Spillikins after supper?'

Araminta still felt annoyed, and apprehensive as well, but that didn't prevent her from enjoying her meal. Jet sent in garlic mushrooms, chicken à la king with braised celery, and then a chocolate mousse. It would be a pity to miss these delights, reflected Araminta, relishing the last of the mousse. She must keep a curb on her tongue in future.

She went back to sit with the boys and the doctor went away to eat his dinner, urged to be quick so that there would be time for one more game of Spillikins before their bedtime.

'It's already past your bedtime,' said Araminta.

'Just for once shall we bend the rules?' said the doctor as he went out of the room.

He was back within half an hour, and another half an hour saw the end of their game. He got up from Paul's bed.

'I'll be back in five minutes,' he told them, 'and you'll both be asleep.'

When he came back he said, 'Thank you, Miss Pomfrey, goodnight.'

She had already tucked the boys in, so she wished him a quiet goodnight and left him there.

A faint grizzling sound wakened her around midnight. Peter had woken up with a headache and a sore throat...

She went down to breakfast in the morning feeling rather the worse for wear. The doctor glanced up briefly from his post, wished her good morning and resumed his reading. Araminta sat down, poured her coffee, and, since he had nothing further to say, observed, 'Peter has the mumps.'

The doctor took off his spectacles, the better to look at her.

'To be expected. I'll go and have a look at him. He had a bad night?'

'Yes,' said Araminta, and stopped herself just in time from adding, And so did I.

'And so did you,' said the doctor, reading her peevish face like an open book. He passed her the basket of rolls and offered butter. 'You'll feel better when you've had your breakfast.'

Araminta buttered a roll savagely. She might have known better than to have expected any sympathy.

She thought of several nasty remarks to make, but he was watching her from his end of the table and for once she decided that prudence might be the best thing.

She bit into her roll with her splendid teeth, choked on a crumb and had to be thumped on the back while she whooped and spluttered. Rather red in the face, she resumed her breakfast and the doctor his seat.

He said mildly, 'You don't appear to be your usual calm self, Miss Pomfrey. Perhaps I should get extra help while the boys are sick.'

'Quite unnecessary,' said Araminta. 'With both of them in bed there will be very little to do.'

She was aware that she was being optimistic; there would be a great deal to do. By the end of the day she would probably be at her wits' end, cross-eyed and sore-throated from reading aloud, headachey from jigsaw puzzles and worn out by coaxing two small fractious boys to swallow food and drink which they didn't want...

'Just as you wish,' observed the doctor, and gathered up his letters. 'I'll go and have a look at Peter. Did Paul sleep?'

'For most of the night.'

He nodded and left her to finish her breakfast, and presently, when he had seen Paul, he returned to tell her that Peter was likely to be peevish and out of sorts. 'I'll give you something before I leave to relieve his sore throat. Paul is getting on nicely. Bas will know how to get hold of me if you are worried. Don't hesitate if you are. I'll be home around six.'

The day seemed endless, but away from the doctor's inimical eye Araminta was her practical, unflappable self, full of sympathy for the two small boys. Naturally they were cross, given to bursts of crying, and unwilling to swallow drinks and the ice cream she offered. Still, towards teatime she could see that Paul was feeling better, and although Peter's temperature was still too high, he was less peevish.

She hardly left them; Nel relieved her when she had a meal, and offered to sit with them while she went out for a while, but Araminta, with Bas translating, assured her that she was fine and that when the doctor came home she would have an hour or two off.

She was reading *The Lion, the Witch and the Wardrobe* when he walked into the room. He sat down on Paul's bed and didn't speak for a moment.

'I see Paul's feeling better; what about Peter?'

He could at least have wished her good evening or even said hello.

'He's feeling off colour, and he's been very good— they both have—and they've taken their drinks like Trojans. Jet is making them jelly for supper.'

'Splendid. Go and have a stroll round the garden, Miss Pomfrey, and then have dinner.'

'I'm perfectly…' she began.

'Yes, I know you are, but kindly do as I say.' He

said something in Dutch to the boys, and they managed to giggle despite the mumps.

Araminta went. First to her room to get a cardigan, and to take a dispirited look at her reflection. There seemed no point in doing more than brushing her hair into tidiness and powdering her nose; she went downstairs and passed Humphrey on his way up to join his master. She would have liked his company as she wandered to and fro in the garden.

It was growing chilly and she was glad of the cardigan and even more glad when Bas came to tell her that dinner would be ready in five minutes.

It was a delicious meal, but she didn't linger over it. The doctor would need his dinner, too, and probably he had plans for his evening. It was Bas who insisted that she went to the drawing room to have her coffee.

Sitting by the cheerful fire presently, with the tray on a table beside her, she felt at peace with everyone…

She was pouring her second cup when she heard Bas admit someone. A minute later the door was thrust open and Christina Lutyns pushed past him and came into the room.

Araminta put the coffeepot down carefully. Her polite 'Good evening, *Mevrouw*,' went unanswered, though.

'Why are you sitting here in the drawing room? Where is Dr van der Breugh? Why aren't you looking after the children?'

Araminta didn't need to answer, for the doctor had come into the room. His '*Dag*, Christina,' was uttered quietly, and he smiled a little. 'Miss Pomfrey is taking a well-earned hour or so from her duties. The reason she is not with the children is because she has been with them almost constantly since the early hours of today. They both have the mumps.'

Christina gave a small shriek. She lapsed into Dutch. 'Don't come near me; I might get them too. And that girl sitting there, she shouldn't be here; she should stay with the boys. I shall go away at once.' She contrived to look tearful. 'And I was looking forward to our evening together. How long will they be ill?'

'Oh, quite a while yet,' said the doctor cheerfully. 'But both Miss Pomfrey and I have had mumps as children, so we aren't likely to get them again.'

'I shall go,' said Christina. 'When there is no more infection you will tell me and we will enjoy ourselves together.'

She went then, ignoring Araminta, escorted to the door by the doctor who showed her out, taking care, at her urgent request, not to get too near to her.

When he went back into the drawing room Araminta had drunk her coffee and was on her feet. She said politely, 'I enjoyed my dinner, thank you. I'll see to the boys now.'

He nodded in an absent-minded manner. 'Yes, yes, by all means. I'll be back later on.'

'There is no need—' began Araminta, then she

caught his eye and ended lamely, 'Very well, doctor,' and went meekly upstairs.

She had the boys ready for bed when he came back upstairs, bade her a civil goodnight, waited while she tucked the boys up and hugged them and then held the door open for her. As she went past him, he told her that he would be away from home for the next two days.

'Unavoidable, I'm afraid, but I have asked a colleague of mine to call in each day. The boys have met him on previous visits and they like him. Don't hesitate to call upon him if you need advice.'

Getting ready for bed, Araminta supposed that she should be glad that the doctor would be away from home. They didn't get on and he was indifferent to her, although she had to admit that he was thoughtful for her comfort, while at the same time indifferent to her as a person.

'Not that I mind,' said Araminta, talking to herself, lying half-sleep in the bath. She said it again to convince herself.

Paul was much better in the morning and Peter, although still sorry for himself, was amenable to swallowing his breakfast. The doctor had left very early, Bas told her, but Dr van Vleet would be calling at about ten o'clock to see the boys.

They were sitting up in their beds, well enough now to talk while Araminta tidied the room, when the doctor came.

He was young, thickset and of middle height with

a rugged face which just missed being handsome, but he had bright blue eyes and a wide smile. He shook hands with her, said something to the boys which made them laugh and added in English, 'Van Vleet— I expect Marcus told you that I would look in.'

'Yes, he did. They're both much better. Peter's still got a slight temperature, but the swellings have gone down since yesterday.'

'I'll take a look…'

Which he did, sitting on their beds while he examined them in turn, talking all the time, making them laugh.

'They're fine. I should think they might get up tomorrow. Though they must stay in a warm room…'

'There's a nursery close by. They could spend the day there.'

'Don't let them get tired.' He smiled nicely at her. 'Marcus told me that you were very experienced with small children, so I don't have to bother you with a great many instructions.'

He closed his bag just as Bas came in. 'Coffee is in the drawing room, Miss Pomfrey, Doctor…Nel will come and stay with the boys while you drink it.'

And when Araminta hesitated, he added, 'Dr van der Breugh instructed me.'

So they went downstairs together and spent a short time over their coffee. Too short, thought Araminta, bidding him goodbye. She liked Dr van Vleet and he seemed to like her. It had been delightful to talk to someone who didn't treat her with indifference, who actually appeared to like talking to her. She was glad that he would be coming again in the morning.

The boys were so much better the next day that there was really no need for Dr van Vleet to call, but he came, looked down their throats, peered into their ears, examined the receding mumps and pronounced himself satisfied.

'Marcus will be back tonight,' he told her. 'I'll phone him in the morning, but will you tell him that the boys are both fine.'

They had coffee together again, and when he got up he asked, 'Do you get time off? I'd like to show you something of Utrecht while you're here.'

Araminta beamed at him. 'I'd like that. I get time off, of course, but it has to fit in with Dr van der Breugh.'

He took out his pocket book and wrote in it. 'Here's my phone number. When you are free, will you phone me? Perhaps we could arrange something.'

'Thank you, I'll let you know.'

She smiled at him, her eyes sparkling at the prospect of a day out with someone with whom she felt so completely at ease.

The pleasant feeling that she had met someone who liked her—enough to ask her out for a whole day—made the day suddenly become perfect, her chores no trouble at all, the boys little angels...

The glow of her pleasure was still in her face when the doctor came home. He had come silently into the house as he so often did, to be welcomed by

Humphrey. Bas hurried to greet him, offered tea or coffee, and took his overnight bag. The doctor went into his study, put away his bag, tossed his jacket on a chair and went upstairs two at a time, to pause in the open doorway of the nursery where the two boys and Araminta were crouched on the floor before a cheerful fire playing Happy Families.

They looked round as he went in and the boys rushed to greet him. Araminta got to her feet and he stared at her for a long moment. He had thought about her while he had been away, unwillingly, aware that she disturbed him in some way, and he had returned home determined to relegate her to where she belonged—the vague background, which he didn't allow to interfere with his work.

But the face she turned to him wasn't easily dismissed; she looked happy. He was so accustomed to her quiet face and self-effacing manner that he was taken aback. Surely that look wasn't for him? He dismissed the idea as absurd and knew it to be so as he watched the glow fade and her features assume their usual calm.

He wished her good evening, listened while she gave him a report on the boy's progress, expressed himself satisfied and, when Bas came to tell him that he had taken his coffee to the drawing room, bore the two boys downstairs with him.

'Fetch them in an hour, if you will, Miss Pomfrey. When they are in bed we can discuss their progress.'

Left alone, she tidied up the room, got everything

ready for bedtime and sat down by the fire. Why was a fire so comforting? she wondered. The house was already warm but there were handsome fireplaces in the rooms in which fires were lighted if a room was in use. She had got used to living in comfort and she wondered now how she would like hospital life.

In a few weeks now they would be returning to England. She thought of that with regret now that she had met Dr van Vleet. She wondered if she should ask for a day off—she was certainly entitled to one— but Dr van der Breugh hadn't looked very friendly— indeed, the look he had given her had made her vaguely uncomfortable…

She fetched the boys presently, and once they were finally in their beds went to her room to change for the evening. The skirt and one of the blouses, she decided. There seemed little point in dressing up each evening, for the doctor was almost never home. But she felt that if Bas took the trouble to set the table with such care, and Jet cooked such delicious dinners for her, the least she could do was to live up to that. She heard the doctor come upstairs and go into the boys' room, and presently, making sure that they were on the verge of sleep, and with a few minutes so spare before Bas came to tell her dinner was ready, she went downstairs.

There was no sign of the doctor, but she hadn't expected to see him. He would probably tell her at breakfast of any plans for the boys. Bas, crossing the hall, opened the drawing room door for her and she went in.

The doctor was sitting in his chair, with Humphrey at his feet. He got up as she went in, offered her a chair, offered sherry and when he sat down again, observed, 'I think we may regard Peter and Paul as being almost back to normal. I think we should keep them from school for another few days, but I see no reason why they shouldn't have a short brisk walk tomorrow if the weather is fine. Children have astonishing powers of recovery.'

Araminta agreed pleasantly and sipped her sherry. She hoped he wasn't going to keep her for too long; she was hungry and it was already past the dinner hour.

'You must have a day to yourself,' said the doctor. 'I'm booked up for the next two days, but after that I will be at home, if you care to avail yourself of a day. And this time I promise to make sure that you enjoy yourself. You may have the Jaguar and a driver, and if you will let me know where you would like to go, I will arrange a suitable tour for you.'

Araminta took another sip of sherry. So she was to be given a treat, was she? Parcelled up and put in a car and driven around like a poor old relative who deserved a nice day out.

She tossed back the rest of the sherry and sat up straight. 'How kind,' she said in a voice brittle with indignation, 'but there is no need of your thoughtful offer. I have other plans.'

The doctor asked carelessly, 'Such as?' and when she gave him a chilly look he said, 'I do stand, as it were, *in loco parentis*.'

'I am twenty-three years old, doctor,' said Araminta in a voice which should have chilled him to the bone.

He appeared untouched. 'You don't look it. Had I not known, I would have guessed nineteen, twenty at the most.' He smiled, and she knew that she would have to tell him.

'Dr van Vleet has asked me to spend the day with him.'

She had gone rather red, so that she frowned as she spoke.

'Ah, a most satisfactory arrangement. And it absolves me from the need to concern myself over you. Telephone him and make any arrangements you like; I am sure you will enjoy yourself with him.' He put down his glass. 'Shall we go in to dinner?'

'Oh, are you going to be here?' Araminta paused; she had put that rather badly. 'What I meant was, you're dining at home this evening?'

The doctor said gravely, 'That is my intention, Miss Pomfrey.' She didn't see his smile, for she was looking at her feet and wondering if she should apologise.

He, aware of that, maintained a steady flow of small talk throughout the meal so that by the time they had finished she felt quite her normal calm self again.

Getting ready for bed later, she even decided that the doctor could, if he chose, be a pleasant companion.

The next few days went well. The boys, making the most of their last free days before going back to school, took her about the city, spending their pocket money, feeding the ducks in the park, taking her to the Oudegracht to look at the ancient stone—a legendary edifice which, they told her, with suitable embellishments, had to do with the devil.

She saw little of the doctor, just briefly at breakfast, with occasional glimpses as he came and went during the day, but never in the evenings. Somehow he made time to be with his nephews before their bedtime, when she was politely told that she might do whatever she wished for a couple of hours, but they didn't dine together again.

Not that Araminta minded. She had phoned Dr van Vleet and, after gaining the doctor's indifferent consent, had agreed to spend the day with him on the following Saturday.

She worried as to what she should wear. It was too chilly for the two-piece; it would have to be a blouse and skirt and the jacket. A pity, she reflected crossly, that she never had the time to go shopping. In the meantime she would have to make do with whatever her meagre wardrobe could produce. She had money, the doctor was punctilious about that, so the very first morning she had an hour or two to herself she would go shopping.

The sun was shining when Dr van Vleet came for her; the doctor had already breakfasted, spent a brief time in his study and was in the garden with the boys, but they all came to see her off, the boys noisily begging her to come back soon. 'As long as you're here in the morning when we wake up,' said Peter.

Dr van Vleet drove a Fiat and she quickly discovered that he liked driving fast. 'Where are we going?' she wanted to know.

'To Arnhem first. We go through the Veluwe— that's pretty wooded country—and at Arnhem there's an open-air village museum you might like to see. You've seen nothing of Holland yet?''

'Well, no, though I've explored Utrecht pretty thoroughly. With the boys.'

'Nice little chaps, aren't they?' He gave her a smiling glance. 'My name's Piet, by the way. And what is it the boys call you?'

'Mintie. Short for Araminta.'

'Then I shall call you Mintie.'

He was right, the Veluwe was beautiful: its trees glowing with autumn colours, the secluded villas half hidden from the road. They stopped for coffee and, after touring the village at Arnhem, had lunch there.

After lunch he drove to Nijmegen and on to Culemborg, and then north to Amersfoort and on to Soestdijk so that she could see the royal palace.

They had tea in Soest and then drove back to Appeldoorn to look at the palace there. Piet finally took the Utrecht road, and she said, 'You've given me a lovely day. I can't begin to thank you; I've loved every minute of it…'

'It's not over yet. I hope you'll have dinner with me. There's rather a nice hotel near Utrecht— Auberge de Hoefslag. Very pretty surroundings, woods all round and excellent food.'

'It sounds lovely, but I'm not dressed…' began Araminta.

'You look all right to me.'

And she need not have worried; the restaurant was spread over two rooms, one modern, the other de- lightfully old-fashioned, and in both there was a fair sprinkling of obvious tourists.

The food was delicious and they didn't hurry over it. By the time they had driven the ten kilometres to Utrecht it was almost eleven o'clock.

Piet got out of the car with her and went with her to the door, waiting while she rang the bell, rather worried as it was later than she had intended. Bas opened the door, beamed a greeting at her and ush- ered her inside. He wished Dr van Vleet a civil good- night and shut the door, and just for a moment Araminta stood in the hall, remembering her happy day and smiling because before they had said good- night he had asked her to go out with him again.

'A happy day, miss?' asked Bas. 'You would like coffee or tea?'

'A lovely day, Bas.' Her eyes shone just thinking about it. 'I don't want anything, thank you. I do hope I haven't kept you up?'

'No, miss. Goodnight.'

She crossed the hall to the staircase. The doctor's study door was half open and she could see him at his desk. He didn't look up, and after a moment's pause she went on up the stairs. He must have heard her come in but he had given no sign. She wouldn't admit it, but her lovely day was a little spoilt by that.

At breakfast he asked her if she had enjoyed her day out, and, quite carried away by the pleasure, she assured him that she had and embarked on a brief description of where they had been, only to realise very quickly that he wasn't in the least interested. So she stopped in mid-sentence, applied herself to attending to the boys' wants and her own breakfast, and when he got up from the table with a muttered excuse took no notice.

He turned back at the door to say, 'I see no reason why the boys shouldn't attend church this morning. Kindly have them ready in good time, Miss Pomfrey. And, of course, yourself.'

So they went to church, the boys delighted to be with their uncle, she at her most staid. The sermon seemed longer than ever, but she didn't mind, she was planning her new clothes. Piet had said he would take her to Amsterdam, a city worthy of a new outfit.

The doctor, sitting so that he could watch her face, wondered why he had considered her so plain—something, someone had brought her to life. He frowned; he must remember to warn her...

There was a general upsurge of the congregation and presently they were walking home again.

They had just finished lunch and were full of ideas as to how they might spend their afternoon when Christina Lutyns was ushered in.

She kissed the doctor on both cheeks, nodded to the boys and ignored Araminta, breaking into a torrent of Dutch.

The doctor had got up as she entered, and stood smiling as she talked. When she paused he said something to make her smile, and then said in English, 'I shall be out for the rest of the day, Miss Pomfrey.' When the boys protested, he promised that when he came home he would be sure to wish them goodnight. 'Although you may be asleep,' he warned them.

They had been asleep for hours when he came home. He went to their room and bent to kiss them and tuck the bedclothes in, and Araminta, who had had a difficult time getting them to go to sleep, hoped that he would have a good excuse in the morning.

Whatever it was, it satisfied the boys, but not her, for he spoke Dutch.

That evening he asked her when she would like her free day. Piet had suggested Thursday, but she felt uncertain of having it. If the doctor had work to do he wouldn't change that to accommodate her. But it seemed that Thursday was possible. 'Going out with van Vleet again?' asked the doctor casually.

'Yes, to Amsterdam.' She added, in a voice which

dared him to disagree with her, 'I hear it is a delightful city. I am looking forward to seeing it.'

'Miss Pomfrey, there is something I should warn you about...'

'Is there? Could it wait, Doctor? The boys will be late for school if I don't take them now.'

'Just as you like, Miss Pomfrey.' And somehow she contrived not to be alone with him for the rest of the day; she felt sure he was going to tell her that they would be returning to England sooner than he had expected, and she didn't want to hear that. Not now that she had met Piet.

Rather recklessly she went shopping during the morning hours while the boys were in school. Clothes, good clothes, she discovered, were expensive, but she couldn't resist buying a dress and loose jacket in a fine wool. It was in pale amber, an impractical colour and probably she wouldn't have much chance to wear it, but it gave her mousy hair an added glint and it was a perfect fit. She bought shoes, too, and a handbag and a pretty scarf.

Thursday came and, much admired by the boys, she went downstairs to meet Piet. He was in the hall talking to the doctor and turned to watch her as she came towards them. His hello was friendly. 'How smart you look—I like the colour; it suits you.'

'We told her that she looks beautiful,' said Peter.

'She does, doesn't she, Uncle?' Paul added.

The doctor, appealed to, observed that indeed Miss

Pomfrey looked charming. But his eyes when he glanced at her were cold.

Amsterdam was everything that she had hoped for, and Piet took her from one museum to the other, for a trip on the canals, a visit to the Rijksmusee and there they had a quick look at the shops. They had coffee and had a snack lunch and, later, tea. And in the evening, as the lights came on, they strolled along the *grachten*, looking at the old houses and the half-hidden antique shops.

He took her to the Hotel de L'Europe for dinner, and it was while they drank their coffee that he told her that he was to marry in the New Year.

'Anna is in Canada, visiting her grandparents,' he told her. 'I miss her very much, but soon she will be home again. You would like each other. She is like you, I think, rather quiet—I think you say in English, a home bird? She is a splendid cook and she is fond of children. We shall be very happy.'

He beamed at her across the table and she smiled back while the half-formed daydreams tumbled down into her new shoes. She had been a fool, but, thank heaven, he had no idea...

'Tell me about her,' said Araminta. Which he did at some length, so that it was late by the time they reached the doctor's house.

'We must go out together again,' said Piet eagerly.

'Well, I'm not sure about that. I believe we're going back to England very shortly. Shall I let you know?' She offered a hand. 'It's been a lovely day, and thank you so very much for giving me dinner. If we don't see each other again, I hope that you and your Anna will be very happy.'

'Oh, we shall,' he assured her.

'Don't get out of the car,' said Araminta. 'There's Bas at the door.'

It was quiet in the hall, and dimly lit. Bas wished her goodnight and went away, and she stood there feeling very alone. She had only herself to thank, of course. Had she really imagined that someone as uninteresting as herself could attract a man? He had asked her out of kindness—she hoped he hadn't pitied her...

She was aware that the study door was open and the doctor was standing there watching her. She made for the stairs, muttering goodnight, but he put out an arm and stopped her.

'You look as though you are about to burst into tears. You'll feel better if you talk about it.'

'I haven't anything to talk about...'

He put a vast arm round her shoulders. 'Oh, yes, you have. I did try to warn you, but you wouldn't allow me to.'

He sounded quite different: kind, gentle and understanding.

'I've been such a fool,' began Araminta as she laid her head against his shoulder and allowed herself the luxury of a good cry.

CHAPTER SIX

THE doctor, waiting patiently while Araminta snivelled and snorted into his shoulder, became aware of several things: the faint scent of clean mousy hair under his chin, the slender softness of her person and a wholly unexpected concern for her. Presently he gave her a large white handkerchief.

'Better?' he asked. 'Mop up and give a good blow and tell me about it.'

She did as she was told, but said in a watery voice, 'I don't want to talk about it, thank you.' And then she added, 'So sorry…' She had slipped from his arm. 'You've been very kind. I'll wash your hanky…'

He sat her down in a small chair away from the brightness of his desk lamp.

'You don't need to tell me if you don't wish to.' He had gone to a small table under the window and come back with a glass. 'Drink that; it will make you feel better.'

She sniffed it. 'Brandy? I've never had any…'

'There's always a first time. Of course, van Vleet told you that he was going to be married shortly.' He watched her sip the brandy and draw a sharp breath at its strength. 'And you had thought that he was interested in you. He should have told you when you first met him, but I imagine that it hadn't entered his head.' He sighed. 'He's a very decent young man.'

Araminta took another sip, a big one, for the brandy was warming her insides. She felt a little sick and at the same time reckless.

She said, in a voice still a little thick from her tears, 'I have been very silly. I should know by now that there is nothing about me to—to make a man interested. I'm plain and I have no conversation, and I wear sensible clothes.'

The doctor hid a smile. 'I can assure you that when you meet a man who will love you, none of these things will matter.'

She said in her matter-of-fact way, 'But I don't meet men—young men. Father and Mother have friends I've known for years. They're all old and mostly married.' She tossed back the rest of the brandy, feeing light-headed. Vaguely she realised that in the morning she was going to feel awful about having had this conversation. 'I shall, of course, make nursing my career and be very successful.' She got to her feet. 'I'll go to bed now.' She made for the door. 'I feel a little sick.'

He crossed the hall with her and stood watching while she made her way upstairs. She looked forlorn and he ignored a wish to help her. Her pride had been shattered; he wouldn't make it worse.

Thanks to the brandy, Araminta slept all night, but everything came rushing back into her head when she woke up. She remembered only too clearly the talk

she had had with the doctor. To weep all over him
had been bad enough, but she had said a great deal
too much. She got up, went to call the boys and
prayed that he would have left the house before they
went down to breakfast.

Her prayers weren't answered; he was sitting at the
table just as usual, reading his letters, his spectacles
perched on his splendid nose.

He got up as they went in, received the boys' hugs
and wished her good morning with his usual cool politeness. She gave him a quick look as she sat down;
there was no sign of the gentle man who had com-
forted her last night. He was as he always was: indifferent, polite and totally uninterested in her. Her
rather high colour subsided; it was clear their conversation was to be a closed book. Well, she had
learned her lesson; if ever a man fell in love with
her—and she doubted that—he would have to prove
it to her in no uncertain fashion. And she would take
care to stay heartwhole.

The day passed in its well-ordered fashion; there
was plenty to keep her occupied. The boys, fit again,
were full of energy, noisy, demanding her attention
and time. She welcomed that, just as she welcomed
the routine, with their uncle's return in the evening
and the hour of leisure while they were with him. He
went out again as soon as they were in bed, wishing
her a cool goodnight as he went.

Araminta, eating her dinner under Bas's kindly eye,
wondered where he was. Probably with Christina

Lutyns, she supposed. Much as she disliked the woman there was no doubt that she would make a suitable wife for the doctor. Suitable, but not the right one. There was a side to him which she had only glimpsed from time to time—not the cool, bland man with his beautiful manners and ease; there was a different man behind that impassive face and she wished she could know that man. A wish not likely to be granted.

The following week wore on, and there had been no mention of her free day. Perhaps he thought she wouldn't want one. It was on Friday evening, when she went to collect the boys at bedtime that he asked her to stay for a moment.

'I don't know if you had any plans of your own, Miss Pomfrey, but on Sunday I'm taking the boys up to Friesland to visit their aunt and uncle. I should say their great-aunt and great-uncle. They live near Leeuwarden, in the lake district, and I think we might make time to take you on a quick tour of the capital. The boys and I would be delighted to have you with us, and my aunt and uncle will welcome you.' His smile was kind. 'You may, of course, wish to be well rid of us!'

It was a thoughtful kindness she hadn't expected. 'I wouldn't be in the way?'

'No. No, on the contrary. I promise you the boys won't bother you, and if you feel like exploring on your own you have only to say so. It would give you

the opportunity of seeing a little more of Holland before we go back to England.'

'Then I'd like to come. Thank you for asking me.
Is it a long drive?'

'Just over a hundred miles. We shall need to leave
soon after eight o'clock; that will give us an hour or
so at Huis Breugh and then after lunch we can spend
an hour in Leeuwarden before going back for tea. The
boys can have their supper when we get back and go
straight to bed.'

Even if she hadn't wanted to go, she would never
have been able to resist the boys' eager little faces.
She agreed that it all sounded great fun and presently
urged them upstairs to baths and bed. When she went
down later it was to find the doctor had gone out. She
hadn't expected anything else, but all the same she
was disappointed.

Which is silly of me, said Araminta to herself, for
he must be scared that I'll weep all over him again.
He must have hated it, and want to forget it as quickly
as possible.

In this she was mistaken. The doctor had admitted
to himself that he had found nothing disagreeable in
Araminta's outburst of crying. True, she had made
his jacket damp, and she had cried like a child, un-
caring of sniffs and snivels, but he hadn't forgotten
any moment of it. Indeed, he had a vivid memory of
the entire episode.

He reminded himself that she would leave his
household in a short while now, and doubtless in a

short time he would have forgotten all about her. In the meantime, however, there was no reason why he shouldn't try and make up for her unhappy little episode with van Vleet.

He reminded himself that he had always kept her at arm's length and would continue to do so. On no account must she be allowed to disrupt his life. His work was his life; he had a wide circle of friends and some day he would marry. The thought of Christina flashed through his mind and he frowned—she would be ideal, of course, for she would allow him to work without trying to alter his life.

He picked up his pen and began making notes for the lecture he was to give that evening.

Araminta, getting up early on Sunday morning, was relieved to see that it was a clear day with a pale blue sky and mild sunshine. She would wear the new dress and jacket and take her short coat with her. That important problem solved, she got the boys dressed and, on going down to breakfast, found the doctor already there.

'It's a splendid day,' he assured them. 'I've been out with Humphrey. The wind is chilly.' He glanced at Araminta. 'Bring a coat with you, Miss Pomfrey.'

'Yes, I will. The boys have their thick jerseys on, but I'll put their jackets in the car. Is Humphrey coming with us?'

'Yes, he'll sit at the back with the boys.'

The boys needed no urging to eat their breakfast,

and a few minutes after eight o'clock they were all in the car, with Bas at the door waving them away.

The doctor took the motorway to Amsterdam and then north to Purmerend and Hoorn and so on to the Afsluitdijk.

'A pity we have no time to stop and look at some of the towns we are passing,' he observed to Araminta. 'Perhaps some other time…'

There wasn't likely to be another time, she reflected, and thrust the thought aside; she was going to enjoy the day and forget everything else. She had told herself sensibly that she must forget about Piet van Vleet. She hadn't been in love with him, but she had been hurt, and was taken by surprise and she was still getting over that. But today's outing was an unexpected treat and she was going to enjoy every minute of it.

Once off the *dijk* the doctor took the road to Leeuwarden and, just past Franeker, took a narrow country road leading south of the city. It ran through farm land: wide fields intersected by narrow canals, grazed by cows and horses. There were prosperous-looking farmhouses and an occasional village.

'It's not at all like the country round Utrecht.'

'No. One has the feeling of wide open spaces here, which in a country as small as Holland seems a solecism. You like it?'

'Yes, very much.'

He drove on without speaking, and when the road

curved through a small copse and emerged on the further side, she could see a lake.

It stretched into the distance, bordered by trees and shrubs. There was a canal running beside it and a narrow waterway leading to a smaller lake. There were sailing boats of every description on it and, here and there, men fishing from its banks, sitting like statues.

The boys were excited now, begging her to look at first one thing, then another. 'Isn't it great?' they wanted to know. 'And it gets better and better. Aren't you glad you came, Mintie?'

She assured them that she was, quite truthfully.

There were houses here and there on the lake's bank, each with its own small jetty, most of them with boats moored there. She didn't like to ask if they were almost there, but she did hope that it might be one of these houses, sitting four-square and solid among the sheltering trees around it.

The doctor turned the car into a narrow brick lane beside a narrow inlet, slowed to go through an open gateway and stopped before a white-walled house with a gabled roof. It had a small square tower to one side and tall chimneys, and it was surrounded by a formal garden. The windows were small, with painted shutters. It was an old house, lovingly maintained, and she could hardly wait to see what it was like inside.

The entrance was at the foot of the tower and led into a small lobby which, in turn, opened into a long wide hall. As they went in two people came to meet them. They were elderly, the man tall and spare, with white hair and still handsome, and the woman with him short and rather stout, with hair which had once been fair and was now silver. In her youth she might have been pretty, and she had beautiful eyes, large and blue with finely marked eyebrows. She was dressed in a tweed skirt and a cashmere twinset in a blue to match her eyes. When she spoke her voice was rather high and very clear.

'Marcus—you're here. I told Bep we would answer the door; she's getting deaf, poor dear.' She stood on tiptoe to receive Marcus's kiss on her cheek and then bent to hug the boys.

'And this is Miss Pomfrey,' said the doctor, and the little lady beamed and clasped Araminta's hand.

'You see I speak English, because I am sure you have no time to speak our language, and it is good practice for me.' Her eyes twinkled. 'We are so glad to meet you, Miss Pomfrey, now you must meet my husband...'

The two men had been greeting each other while the boys stood one each side of them, but now her host came to her and shook her hand.

'You are most welcome, Miss Pomfrey. I hear from Marcus that you are a valued member of his household.'

'Thank you. Well, yes, just for a few weeks.' She smiled up into his elderly face and liked him.

He stared back at her and then nodded his head.

She wondered what he was thinking, and then forgot about it as his wife reminded them that coffee was waiting for them in the drawing room. Araminta, offered a seat by her hostess, saw that the doctor had the two boys with him and his uncle and relaxed.

'Of course, Marcus did not tell you our name? He is such a clever man, with that nose of his always in his books, and yet he forgets the simplest things. I am his mother's sister—of course, you know that his parents are dead, some years ago now—our name is Nos-Wieringa. My husband was born and brought up in this house and we seldom leave it. But we love to see the family when they come to Holland. You have met the boys' mother?'

Araminta said that, yes, she had.

'And you, my dear? Do you have any brothers and sisters and parents?'

'Parents. No brothers or sisters. I wish I had.'

'A family is important. Marcus is the eldest, of course, and he has two younger brothers and Lucy. Of course you know she lives in England now that she is married, and the two boys are both doctors; one is in Canada and the other in New Zealand. They should be back shortly—some kind of exchange posts.'

Mevrouw Nos-Wieringa paused for breath and Araminta reflected that she had learned more about the doctor in five minutes than in the weeks she had been working for him.

Coffee drunk, the men took the boys down to the

home farm, a little distance from the house. There were some very young calves there, explained the doctor, and one of the big shire horses had had a foal.

'And I will show you the house,' said Mevrouw Nos-Wieringa. 'It is very old but we do not wish to alter it. We have central heating and plumbing and electricity, of course, but they are all concealed as far as possible. You like old houses?'

'Yes, I do. My parents live in quite a small house,' said Araminta, anxious not to sail under false pretences. 'It is quite old, early nineteenth-century, but this house is far older than that, isn't it?'

'Part of it is thirteenth-century, the rest seventeenth-century. An ancestor made a great deal of money in the Dutch East Indies and rebuilt the older part.'

The rooms were large and lofty, with vast oak beams and white walls upon which hung a great many paintings.

'Ancestors?' asked Araminta.

'Yes, mine as well as my husband's. All very alike, aren't they? You must have noticed that Marcus has the family nose. Strangely enough, few of the women had it. His mother was rather a plain little thing—the van der Breughs tend to marry plain women. They're a very old family, of course, and his grandfather still lives in the family home. You haven't been there?'

Araminta said that, no, she hadn't, and almost added that it was most unlikely that she ever would. Seeking a change of subject, she admired a large oak pillow cupboard. She mustn't allow her interest in the doctor to swamp common sense.

They lunched presently, sitting at a large oak table on rather uncomfortable chairs; it was a cheerful meal, since the children were allowed to join in the conversation. As they rose from the table Mevrouw Nos-Wieringa said, 'Now, off you go, Marcus, and take Mintie—I may call you Mintie?—with you. We will enjoy having the boys to ourselves for a while, but be back by six o'clock for the evening meal.'

Araminta, taken by surprise, looked at the doctor. He was smiling.

'Ah, yes, it slipped my memory. The boys and I decided that I should take you to Leeuwarden and give you a glimpse of it...'

When she opened her mouth to argue, he said, 'No, don't say you don't want to come; the boys will be disappointed. It was their idea that you should have a treat on your free day.'

The boys chorused agreement. 'We knew you'd like to go with Uncle Marcus. He'll show you the weigh house and the town hall, and there's a little café by the park where you could have tea.'

In the face of their eager pleasure there was nothing she could say.

'It sounds marvellous,' she told them. 'And what dears you are to have thought of giving me a treat.'

In the car presently, driving along the narrow fields towards Leeuwarden, she said stiffly, 'This is kind of you, but it's disrupting your day. You must wish to spend time with your aunt and uncle.'

He glanced at her rather cross face. 'No, no, Miss Pomfrey, I shall enjoy showing you round. Besides, I can come here as often as I wish, but you are not likely to come to Friesland—Holland—again, are you? What free time you get from hospital you will want to spend at your own home.'

She agreed, at the same time surprised to discover that the prospect of hospital was no longer filling her with happy anticipation. She should never have taken this job, she reflected. It had unsettled her—a foreign country, living in comfort, having to see the doctor each day. She rethought that—he might unsettle her, but she had to admit that he had made life interesting...

She asked suddenly, and then could have bitten out her tongue, 'Do you mean to marry Mevrouw Lutyns?' Before he could reply she added, 'I'm sorry, I can't think why I asked that. It was just—just an idle thought.'

He appeared unsurprised. 'Do you think that I should?' He added pleasantly, 'Feel free to speak your mind, Miss Pomfrey. I value your opinion.'

This astonished her. 'Do you? Do you really? Is it because I'm a stranger—a kind of outside observer? Though I don't suppose you would take any notice of what I say.'

'Very likely not.'

'Well, since you ask... Mevrouw Lutyns is very

beautiful, and she wears lovely clothes—you know, they don't look expensive but they are, and they fit. Clothes off the peg have to be taken up or let out or hitched up, and that isn't the same…'

They were on the outskirts of Leeuwarden, and she watched the prosperous houses on either side of the street. 'This looks a nice place.'

'It is. Answer my question, Miss Pomfrey.'

'Well…' Why must she always begin with 'well'? she wondered. Her mother would say it was because she was a poor conversationalist. 'I think that perhaps you wouldn't be happy together. I imagine that she has lots of friends and likes going out and dancing and meeting people, and you always have your nose in a book or are going off to some hospital or other.' She added suddenly, 'I'm sure I don't know why you asked me this; it's none of my business.' She thought for a moment. 'You would make a handsome pair.'

The doctor turned a laugh into a cough. 'I must say that your opinion is refreshing.'

'Yes, but it isn't going to make any difference.'

He didn't answer but drove on into the inner city and parked the car by the weigh house. 'I should have liked to take you to the Friesian Museum, but if I do there will be no time to see anything of the city. We will go to the Grote Kerk first, and then the Oldehove Tower, and then walk around so that you may see some of the townhouses. They are rather fine…'

He took her from here to there, stopping to point out an interesting house, the canals and bridges, interesting gables, and the town hall. Araminta gazed around, trying to see everything at once, determined to remember it all.

'Now we will do as the boys suggested and have tea—there is the café. They remember it because it has such a variety of cakes. We had better sample some or they will be disappointed.'

It was a charming place, surrounded by a small lawn and flowerbeds which even in autumn were full of colour. The tea was delicious, pale and weak, with no milk, but she was thirsty and the dish of cakes put before them were rich with cream and chocolate and crystallised fruit. Araminta ate one with a simple pleasure and, pressed to do so, ate another.

The doctor, watching her enjoyment, thought briefly of Christina, who would have refused for fear of adding a few ounces to her slimness. Araminta appeared to have no such fear. She was, he conceded silently, a very nice shape.

'That was a lovely tea,' said Araminta, walking back to the car. 'I've had a marvellous afternoon. Thank you very much. And your aunt and uncle have been very kind.'

He made a vague, casual answer, opened the car door for her and got in beside her. When she made some remark about the street they were driving along, he gave a non-committal reply so that she concluded that he didn't want to talk. Perhaps he felt that he had done his duty and could now revert to his usual manner. So she sat silently until they had reached the house, and then there was no need to be silent, for the boys wanted to know if she had enjoyed herself, what she had thought of Leeuwarden and, above all, what kind of cakes she had had for tea.

She was glad of their chatter, for it filled the hour or so before they sat down to their meal. They had had a wonderful afternoon, she was told. They had fished in the lake with their great-uncle, and gone with their great-aunt to see the kitchen cat with her kittens—and did she know that there were swans on the lake and that they had seen a heron?

She made suitable replies to all this and then sat with Mevrouw Nos-Wieringa and listened to that lady's gentle flow of talk. There was no need to say anything to the doctor, and really there was no need even to think of that, for he went away with his uncle for a time to look at something in the study, and when they came back they were bidden to the table.

As a concession to the boys, the meal was very similar to an English high tea, and the food had been chosen to please them, finishing with a plate of *poffertjes*—small balls of choux pastry smothered in fine sugar. Araminta enjoyed them as much as the boys.

They left soon afterwards. The boys eager to come again with their mother and father, the doctor saying that he would spend a weekend with his aunt and uncle when next he came to Holland. Araminta, saying all the right things, wished very much that she would be coming again, too.

The boys were tired by now, and after a few

minutes of rather peevish wrangling they dozed off, leaning against Humphrey's bulk. The doctor drove in silence, this time travelling back via Meppel and Zwolle, Hardewijk and Hilversum, so that Araminta might see as much of Holland as possible.

He told her this in a disinterested manner, so that she felt she shouldn't bother him with questions. She sat quietly, watching his large capable hands on the wheel, vaguely aware that she was unhappy.

It was dark by the time they reached Utrecht, and she urged the sleepy boys straight up to bed with the promise of hot milk and a biscuit once they were there. They were still peevish, and it took time and patience to settle them. She was offering the milk when the doctor came to say goodnight, and when he added a goodnight to her, she realised that he didn't expect her to go downstairs again.

She thanked him for her pleasant day in a damp-ened down voice, since he was obviously impatient to be gone, and when he had, she tucked up the boys and went to her room.

It wasn't late, and she would have liked a cup of tea or a drink of some sort. There was no reason why she shouldn't go down to the kitchen and ask for it, but the thought of encountering him while doing so prevented her. She undressed slowly, had a leisurely bath and got into bed. It had been a lovely day—at least, it would have been lovely if the doctor had been friendly.

She fell asleep presently, still feeling unhappy.

The boys woke early in splendid spirits so that breakfast was a lively meal. The doctor joined in their chatter, but beyond an austere good morning he had nothing to say to Araminta.

It's just as though I'm not here, she reflected, listening to plans being made by the boys to go shopping for presents to take back with them.

'You must buy presents, too,' they told Araminta. 'To take home, you know. We always do. Uncle comes with us so's he can pay when we've chosen.'

'I expect Miss Pomfrey will prefer to do her shopping without us. Let me see, I believe I can spare an afternoon this week.'

'Mintie?' Paul looked anxious.

'Your uncle is quite right; I'd rather shop by myself. But I promise you I'll show you what I've bought and you can help me wrap everything up.'

Suddenly indignant, she suggested that the boys should go and fetch their schoolbooks, and when they had gone she turned her eyes, sparkling with ill temper, on the doctor.

'Presumably we are to return to England shortly?' she enquired in a voice to pulverise a stone. 'It would be convenient for me if you were to be civil enough to tell me when.'

The doctor put down the letter he was reading. 'My dear Miss Pomfrey, you must know by now that I'm often uncivil. If I have ruffled your feelings, I am sorry.' He didn't look in the least sorry, though, merely amused.

'We shall return in five days' time. I have various appointments which I must fulfil but the boys will remain with me until their parents return within the next week or so. I hope that you are agreeable to remain with them until they do? You will, of course, be free to go as soon as their parents are back.'

'You said that you would arrange for me to start my training…'

'Indeed I did, and I will do so. You are prepared to start immediately? Frequently a student nurse drops out within a very short time. If that were the case, you would be able to take her place. I will do what I can for you. You are still determined to take up nursing?'

'Yes. Why do you ask?'

'I'm not sure if the life will suit you.'

'I'm used to hard work,' she told him. 'This kind of life—' she waved a hand around her '—is something I've never experienced before.'

'You don't care for it?'

She gave him an astonished look. 'Of course I like it. I had better go and see if the boys are ready for school.'

That morning she went shopping, buying a scarf for her mother, a book on the history of the Netherlands for her father and a pretty blouse for her cousin, who would probably never wear it. She bought cigars for Bas, too, and another scarf for Jet, and a box of sweets for Nel and the elderly woman who came each day to polish and clean. Mindful of her promise to the boys, she found pretty paper and ribbons. Wrapping everything up would keep them occupied for half an hour at least, after their tea, while they were waiting impatiently for their uncle to come home.

They were still engrossed in this, sitting on the floor in the nursery with Araminta, when the door opened and the doctor and Mevrouw Lutyns came in.

The boys ran to him at once and Araminta got to her feet, feeling at a disadvantage. Mevrouw Lutyns was, as always, beautifully dressed, her face and hair utter perfection. Araminta remembered only too clearly the conversation she had had with the doctor in Leeuwarden and felt the colour creep into her cheeks. How he must have laughed at her. Probably he had shared the joke with the woman.

Mevrouw Lutyns ignored her, greeted the boys in a perfunctory manner and spoke sharply to the doctor. He had hunkered down to tie a particularly awkward piece of ribbon and answered her in a casual way, which Araminta saw annoyed her. He spoke in English, too, which, for the moment at any rate, made her rather like him. A tiresome man, she had to admit, but his manners were beautiful. Unlike Mevrouw Lutyns'.

He glanced at Araminta and said smoothly. 'Mevrouw Lutyns is thinking of coming to England for a visit.'

'I expect you know England well?' said Araminta politely.

'London, of course. I don't care for the country. Besides, I must remain in London. I need to shop.' Her lip curled. 'I don't expect you need to bother with clothes.'

Araminta thought of several answers, all of them rude, so she held her tongue.

The doctor got to his feet. 'Come downstairs to the drawing room, Christina, and have a drink.' And to the boys he added, 'I'll be back again presently— we'll have a card game before bed.'

They went away and Peter whispered. 'We don't like her; she never talks to us. Why does Uncle like her, Mintie?'

'Well, she's very pretty, you know, and I expect she's amusing and makes him laugh, and she wears pretty dresses.'

Paul flung an arm round her. 'We think you're pretty, Mintie, and you make us laugh and wear pretty clothes.'

She gave him a hug. 'Do I really? How nice of you to say so. Ladies like compliments, you know.'

She found a pack of cards. 'How about a game of Happy Families before your uncle comes?'

They were in the middle of a noisy game when he returned. When she would have stopped playing he squatted down beside her.

'One of my favourite games,' he declared, 'and much more fun with four.'

'Has Mevrouw Lutyns gone home?' asked Paul.

'Yes, to dress up for the evening. We are going out to dinner.'

He looked at Araminta as he spoke, but she was shuffling her cards and didn't look up.

Two days later the boys went with their uncle to do their shopping, leaving Araminta to start packing. She had been happy in Holland and she would miss the pleasant life, but now she must concentrate on her future. Her mother, in one of her rare letters, had supposed that she would go straight to the hospital when she left the doctor's house. Certainly she wasn't expected to stay home for any length of time. All the same, she would have to go home for a day or so to repack her things.

'We may be away,' her mother had written. 'There is an important lecture tour in Wales. Your cousin will be here, of course.' She had added, as though she had remembered that Araminta was her daughter, whom she loved, 'I am glad you have enjoyed your stay in Holland.'

Neither her mother or her father would be interested in her life there, nor would her cousin, and there would scarcely be time for her to look up her friends. There would be no one to whom she could describe the days she had spent in the doctor's house. Just for a moment she gave way to self-pity, and then reminded herself that she had a worthwhile future before her despite the doctor's doubts.

For the last few days before they left she saw almost nothing of the doctor. The boys, excited at the prospect of going back to England, kept her busy, and they spent the last one or two afternoons walking the, by now, well known streets, pausing at the bridges to stare down into the canals, admiring the boatloads of flowers and, as a treat, eating mountainous ices in one of the cafés.

They were to leave early in the morning, and amidst the bustle of departure Araminta had little time to feel sad at leaving. She bade Jet and Bas goodbye, shook hands with Nel and the daily cleaner, bent to hug Humphrey, saw the boys settled on the back seat and got in beside the doctor.

It was only as he drove away that she allowed herself to remember that she wouldn't be coming again. In just a few weeks she had come to love the doctor's house, and Utrecht, its pleasant streets and small hidden corners where time since the Middle Ages had stood still. I shall miss it, she thought and then, I shall miss the doctor, too. Once she had left his house she wasn't likely to see him again. There was no chance of their lives converging; he would become part of this whole interlude. An important part.

I do wonder, thought Araminta, how one can fall in love with someone who doesn't care a row of pins for one, for that's what I have done. And what a good thing that I shall be leaving soon and never have to see him again.

The thought brought tears to her eyes and the doctor, glancing sideways at her downcast profile, said kindly, 'You are sorry to be leaving Holland, Miss

Pomfrey? Fortunately it is not far from England and you will be able to pay it another visit at some time.'

Oh, no, I won't, thought Araminta, but murmured in agreement.

Their journey was uneventful. They arrived back at his London home to be welcomed by Briskett, with tea waiting. It was as though they had never been away.

CHAPTER SEVEN

BRISKETT handed the doctor his post, informed him that there were a number of phone calls which needed to be dealt with at once, took the boys' jackets and invited Araminta to go with him so that he might show her to her room.

'The boys' are in their usual room. They'd better come with you, miss; the doctor won't want to be bothered for a bit. Had a good time, have you? Hope the boss took time off to show you round a bit.'

'Well, yes, we went to Friesland.'

He turned to smile at her, his cheerful rat face split in a wide smile. 'Nice to have him back again, miss. Here's your room. Make yourself at home.'

It would be difficult not to feel at home in such a delightful room, thought Araminta, with its satinwood bed, tall chest and dressing table. The curtains and bedspread were white and pale yellow chintz, and someone had put a vase of freesias by the bed. The window overlooked the long narrow garden, with a high brick wall and trees screening it from its neighbours.

She would have liked to linger there, but the boys would need to be seen to. They had been good on the journey, but now they were tired and excited. Tea and an early bedtime were indicated, unless the doctor had other plans. She went to their room, tidied them up and took them downstairs.

The study, where she had first been interviewed by the doctor, had its door open. The doctor was at his desk, sitting back in his chair, on the phone, and speaking in Dutch. Araminta's sharp ears heard that. He looked up as they went past.

'Go into the sitting room. Briskett will have tea waiting. I'll join you presently.'

So the boys led her across the hall into quite a small room, very cosy, where Briskett was putting the finishing touches to the tea table.

'I've laid a table,' he told her. 'I don't hold with little nippers balancing plates on their knees. Just you sit down, miss, and I'll give the boss a call.'

The doctor joined them presently, ate a splendid tea and then excused himself with the plea of work. 'I have to go out,' he told the boys, 'and I don't think I'll be back before you go to bed, but I'm not doing anything tomorrow morning; we will go to the park and feed the ducks.' He glanced at Araminta. 'I'm sure Miss Pomfrey will be glad of an hour or two to get your clothes unpacked.' He added casually, 'I expect you would like to let your parents know you are back in England; do ring them if you wish.'

She thanked him. 'And, if you don't mind, I'll go and unpack the boys' night things. I thought an early bedtime…'

'Very wise. I'm sure Briskett will have something extra special for their supper.'

'Perhaps I could have my supper at the same time with them?'

'You would prefer that? Then by all means do so. I'll let Briskett know. You'll bathe them and have them ready for bed first? Shall I tell him seven o'clock?'

'That would do very well, thank you.' She hesitated. 'Are you going out immediately? If you are, then I'll wait and unpack later.'

He glanced at his watch. 'Half an hour or so, but I need to change first.'

'If I can have ten minutes?'

'Of course.'

She unpacked the overnight bag, put everything ready in the boys' bathroom and whisked herself back downstairs with a minute to spare. The doctor bade the boys goodnight, nodded to her and went away. She was in the boy's room, which overlooked the street, when she heard him in the hall and went to look out of the window. He was getting into his car, wearing black tie, looking remarkably handsome.

'I wonder when he gets any work done,' reflected Araminta. 'Talk about a social whirl.' She knew that wasn't fair, he worked long hours and he was good at it, but it relieved her feelings. She hoped lovingly that he wouldn't stay out too late; he needed his sleep like anyone else...

She sighed; she had managed all day not to think

too much about him and it had been made easier by his distant manner towards her, but loving him was something she couldn't alter, even though it was hopeless. No one died of a broken heart; they went on living like everyone else and made a success of their lives. Something which she was going to do. But first she must learn to forget him, once she had left his house. Until then, surely it wouldn't do any harm if she thought about him occasionally?

The boys came tumbling in then, and she allowed stern common sense to take over.

Life in London would be very different from that of Utrecht. For one thing there would be no school in the mornings.

Their parents would be returning in a few days now, and the boys were excited and full of high spirits; she filled the mornings with simple lessons and the afternoons with brisk walks, returning in time for tea and games before bedtime. The doctor was seldom at home; as Briskett put it, 'Up early and home late. No time for anything but his work. Good thing he's got a bit of social life of an evening. You know what they say, miss, "All work and no play"...'

But the doctor still found time to spend an hour with the boys each evening, although it was very evident that he had no time for Araminta. His brief good mornings and good evenings were the extent of his conversations with her. And what else did she expect? she asked herself.

They had been back in England for three days before he told her that the boys' parents would be arriving in two days time.

'Perhaps you would be good enough to remain for a day or so after their return; my sister is bound to wish to talk to you, and their clothes and so on will need to be packed up. She will be glad of your help.'

Three days, thought Araminta, four at the outside, and after that I shan't see him again. 'Of course I'll stay on, if Mrs Ingram wishes me to,' she told him.

She was surprised when he asked, 'You will go home? Your people expect you?'

'Yes.' She didn't add that they would probably still be away. Her cousin would be there, of course, and she supposed she would stay there until she heard from the hospital. Which reminded her to add, 'You told me that there was a chance that I might be accepted at the hospital...'

'Ah, yes. It slipped my memory. There is indeed a vacancy; one of the students has left owing to illness. If you can start within a few days and are prepared to work hard in order to catch up with the other students you will be accepted.'

She should have been elated. He had made everything easy for her; she could embark on her plans for a nursing career. And it had been so unimportant to him that he had forgotten to tell her.

'That is what you wanted?' He had spoken so sharply that she hurried to say that, yes, there was nothing she wished for more.

'I'm very grateful,' she added. 'Is there anything that I should do about it?'

'No, no. You will receive a letter within the next day or two. And you have no need to be grateful. You have been of great help while the boys have been with me. They will miss you.'

The doctor spoke with an austere civility which chilled her, but he was aware as he said it that *he* would miss her too: her small cheerful person around the house, her quiet voice which could on occasion become quite sharp with annoyance. He had a sudden memory of her weeping into his shoulder and found himself thinking of it with tenderness...

He chided himself silently for being a sentimental fool. Miss Pomfrey had fulfilled a much needed want for a few weeks, and he was grateful for that, but once she had gone he would forget her.

Mr and Mrs Ingram duly arrived, late in the afternoon. It was a chilly October day, with a drizzling rain, and Araminta had been hard pushed to keep the boys happy indoors. But at last they shouted to Araminta from their perch by the front windows that their uncle's car had just arrived with their mother and father.

'Then off you go downstairs, my dears. Go carefully.'

She went to the window when they had gone, in time to see Mr and Mrs Ingram enter the house, followed at a more leisurely pace by the doctor. They would all have tea, she supposed, and sat down quietly to wait until Briskett brought her own tea tray. She had sought him out that morning and he had agreed with her that it might be a good idea if she were to have her tea in her room.

'The boys will be so excited, and they will all have so much to talk about that I won't be needed,' she had pointed out.

He came presently with the news that there was a fine lot of talk going on downstairs and she hadn't been missed.

'They'll send for you presently, miss, when they're over the first excitement,' he assured her. 'The boss'll want you there to give a report, as it were.' He gave her a friendly nod. 'Sets great store on you, he does.'

She drank her tea and nibbled at a cake, her usually splendid appetite quite gone. She would start packing this evening, once the boys were in bed, so that when she had done all she could do to help Mrs Ingram, she would be able to leave at once.

She was pouring another cup of tea when the door opened and the doctor came in.

'I didn't hear you knock,' said Araminta in her best Miss Pomfrey voice.

'My apologies. Why did you not come downstairs to tea?'

'It's a family occasion.'

He leaned forward and took a cake and ate it—one of Briskett's light-as-air fairy cakes—and the simple act turned him from a large, self-assured man into a small boy.

Araminta swallowed the surge of love which engulfed her. However would she be able to live without him?

The doctor finished his cake without haste. 'You have finished your tea? Then shall we go downstairs?'

She shot him a look and encountered a bland stare. There was nothing for it but to do as he asked. How is it possible, she thought, to love someone who is so bent on having his own way? She accompanied him downstairs to the drawing room, to be warmly greeted by the boys' parents. Presently Mrs Ingram drew her on one side.

'They were good?' she wanted to know anxiously. 'Peter and Paul can be perfect little horrors…' She said it with love.

'Well, they weren't; they have been really splendid—very obedient and helpful and never bored.'

'Oh, good. I expect you're longing to go home. Could you stay over tomorrow and help me pack their things?'

'Yes, of course. You must be glad to be going home again. I know the boys will be, although they enjoyed living in Utrecht. It seemed like a second home to them.'

'Well, they love Marcus, of course, and since they've both spoken Dutch and English ever since they could utter words they don't feel strange. I'm sure they will have a lot to tell us. You were happy in Holland?'

'Oh, yes. I enjoyed it very much…'

'Marcus tells me that you're to start nursing train-ing very shortly. That's something you want to do?' Mrs Ingram smiled. 'No boyfriend?'

'No, I expect I'm meant to be a career girl!'

If Mrs Ingram had any opinion about that she re-mained silent, and presently Araminta took the boys off to bed and supper, before slipping away to her room while their parents came to say goodnight. This was a lengthy business, with a great deal of giggling and talk until they consented to lie down and go to sleep. Excitement had tired them out; they slept in the instant manner of children and she was free to go to her room and change her dress.

She excused herself as soon as she decently could after dinner; it had been a pleasant meal, and she had borne her part in the conversation when called upon to do so, but although the talk had been general, she had no doubt that her company hindered the other three from any intimate talk.

She was bidden a friendly goodnight and the doctor got up to open the door for her. She went past him without a look and went off to her room and started to pack her things. Tomorrow she knew that she would be kept busy getting the boys' clothes packed. She felt lonely; Humphrey's company would have been welcome, but of course he was miles away in Utrecht. So she was forced to talk to herself.

'I'm perfectly happy,' she assured herself. 'My fu-ture is settled, I have money, I shall make friends with the other nurses, and in a year or two I shall be able to pick and choose where I mean to work.' Not London. The chance of meeting the doctor was remote but, all the same, not to be risked.

There was no one at breakfast when she went down with the boys: the doctor had already left and Mr and Mrs Ingram weren't yet down. They had almost finished when they joined them. Araminta left the boys with them and at Mrs Ingram's suggestion began the task of packing up for the boys. They were to leave that evening but first they were to go shopping with their father and mother. So Araminta had a solitary lunch and spent the afternoon collecting up the boys' toys and tidying them away into various boxes. They were to be driven home by the doctor directly after tea, and she had been asked to have everything ready by then.

Briskett, going round the house retrieving odds and ends for her to pack, was of the opinion that the house would be very dull once they had gone. 'And you'll be leaving, miss—we shall miss you, too. Very quiet, it'll be.'

'I expect the doctor will be quite glad to have the house to himself,' said Araminta.

'Well, now, as to that, I'd venture to disagree, miss. The boss is fond of children and you've fitted in like a glove on a hand.'

She thanked him gravely. He was a kind little man, despite his ratty looks, and he was devoted to the doctor. 'Maybe you'll be back, miss,' said Briskett, to her surprise.

'Me? Oh, I don't think so, Briskett. You mean as a governess when the doctor marries and has children? By then I'll be a trained nurse and probably miles away.'

It took some time for the doctor to get his party settled with their possessions in the car and still longer for them to make their goodbyes. The boys hugged and kissed Araminta and rather silently handed her a parcel, painstakingly wrapped in fancy paper. Seeing the look on their small faces, she begged to be allowed to open it there and then.

'They chose it themselves,' said their mother rather apologetically.

It was a coffret of face cream, powder and lipstick, and a little bottle of scent. When Araminta exclaimed over it, Peter said, 'We know you're not pretty, but these things will make you beautiful. The lady behind the counter said so.'

'It's just exactly what I've always wanted,' declared Araminta, 'and thank you both very much for thinking of such a lovely present. I'll use it every day and I'm sure I'll be beautiful in no time at all.'

She hugged them both, told them to be good boys and then watched with Briskett as they all got into the car, parcels and packages squashed into the back seat with the boys and their mother. They all waved and smiled, but not the doctor, of course; he raised a casual hand as he drove away but he didn't turn his head.

Araminta finished her packing, ate a solitary dinner

and decided to go to bed. There was no sign of the doctor; probably he would stay the night at his sister's house. She was halfway up the stairs when he came in and Briskett appeared in the hall to offer supper.

'No, no, I've had a meal, thanks, Briskett, but will you see to the car? I'll be in my study.'

He glanced at Araminta, poised on the stairs. 'Miss Pomfrey, if you would spare me a few minutes…?'

She went with him to his study and sat down in the chair he offered her.

'You've had the letter from the hospital?' And when she said yes, he went on, 'Briskett will drive you to your home in the morning. I expect you are anxious to get back. Is there anything you want to know about your appointment as a student nurse? I presume you have been given instructions?'

'Yes, thank you. There is no need for Briskett to drive me…'

He said in a level voice, 'If you will just tell him when you are ready to leave, Miss Pomfrey. I shall see you in the morning before you go. I won't keep you now; you must be tired.'

She got up quickly. 'Yes, yes, I am. Goodnight, Doctor.'

His goodnight was very quiet.

She went down to breakfast after a wakeful night to find that the doctor had been called away very early in the morning. 'Not knowing when he'll be back, he said not to wait for him, miss. I'll have the car round as soon as you've had breakfast.'

Araminta crumbled toast onto her plate and drank several cups of coffee. Now she would never say goodbye to the doctor. Possibly he had left the house early, so that he might avoid a last meeting. She had no idea what she had expected from it, but at least she had hoped that they would part in a friendly fashion. She went suddenly hot and cold at the idea that he might have guessed that she had fallen in love with him. Now her one thought was to leave his house as quickly as possible…her one regret that Hambledon wasn't thousands of miles away.

It was almost noon when Briskett drew up before her home, took her case from the boot and followed her up the path to the front door.

'Looks empty,' he observed. 'Expecting you, are they?'

'My mother and father are in Wales on a lecture tour. A cousin is staying here, though—housekeeping now that I'm not at home.'

Briskett took the key from her and opened the door. There were letters on the doormat and an open note on the hall table. His sharp eyes had read it before Araminta had seen it. 'Gone with Maud—' Maud was a friend of Millicent, the cousin '—for a couple of days. Good luck with your new job.'

He was bending over her case as she saw it and read it.

'Where will I put this, miss? I'll take it upstairs for you.'

'Thank you, Briskett. It's the room on the left on

the landing. Will you stay while I make a cup of tea? I'd offer you lunch, but I'm not quite sure…'

'A cuppa would be fine, miss.'

Briskett hefted the case and went upstairs. Nice little house, he decided, and some nice furniture—good old-fashioned stuff, no modern rubbish. But the whole place looked unlived-in, as though no one much bothered about it. He didn't like leaving Miss Pomfrey alone, but she hadn't said anything about the note so he couldn't do much about that.

He went down to the kitchen, again old-fashioned but well equipped, and found her making the tea.

'I've found some biscuits,' she told him cheerfully. 'Will you get back in time to make lunch for yourself?'

'Easy, miss, there won't be all that much traffic.' He eyed Cherub, who had come in though the kitchen window she had opened and was making much of Araminta.

'Nice cat. Yours, is he?'

'Yes, I found him. Have another biscuit. I shall miss Humphrey in Utrecht…'

Briskett's long thin nose quivered. 'I'm sure he'll miss you. Pity the boss wasn't home. Beats me, it does, him at the top of the tree, so to speak, and still working all the hours God made.'

When he had gone Araminta unpacked. Presently she would sort out her clothes and repack, ready to leave the next day, but for now she went to inspect the fridge. Even those with broken hearts needed to be fed.

As the doctor let himself into his house that evening Briskett came into the hall.

'A bit on the late side, aren't you?' he observed. 'Had a busy day, I'll be bound. I've a nice little dinner ready for you.'

'Thanks, Briskett. You took Miss Pomfrey back to her home?'

Briskett nodded. 'There's a nice young lady for you. I didn't fancy leaving her in that empty house.' He met the doctor's sudden blue stare and went on, 'Her ma and pa are in Wales. There's a cousin or some such looking after the house, but she'd gone off for a few days. Only living thing to greet us was a tatty old cat.'

He watched the doctor's face; he really looked quite ferocious but he didn't speak. Briskett reckoned he was pretty angry...

'Nice house,' he went on. 'Small, some nice stuff though, good and solid, a bit old-fashioned. Nice bits of silver and china too.' He paused to think. 'But it weren't a home.'

And, when the doctor still remained silent, 'We had a cuppa together—very concerned, she was, about me not having my dinner.'

'Did Miss Pomfrey tell you that this cousin was away?'

'Not a word. I happened to see the note on the table.'

'She seemed quite happy?'

'Now, as to that, Boss, I wouldn't like to venture an opinion.'

He hesitated, cautious of the doctor's set face. 'I'd have brought her back, but that wouldn't have done, would it?'

'No, Briskett, it wouldn't have done at all. You did right. Miss Pomfrey will be going to St Jules' tomorrow, and I dare say this cousin will have returned by then.'

The doctor went into his study and sat down at his desk, staring at the papers on it, not seeing them. I miss her, he thought. I can't think why. She has no looks, she wears drab clothes, she has at times a sharp tongue and yet her voice is delightful and she is kind and patient and sensible. And she has beautiful eyes.

He drew the papers towards him and picked up his pen. This feeling of loss is only temporary, he mused. She has been a member of the household for some weeks; one gets used to a person. I shall forget her completely in a few weeks.

He went to his solitary dinner then, agreeing with Briskett that it was pleasant to have a quiet house once more. Now he would be able to prepare the notes on the learned treatise he was writing without the constant interference of small boys' voices—and Mintie's voice telling them to hush.

He went to his desk after dinner but he didn't write

a word, his mind occupied with thoughts of Araminta, alone at her home with only a cat for company. There was no use trying to work, so he took himself for a brisk walk and went to bed—but he didn't sleep.

Araminta had had a boiled egg and some rather stale bread for a late lunch, fed Cherub, put on the washing machine and started packing again. She was to report to the hospital at two o'clock the next day and, since there was no indication as to when her cousin would return, she went down the lane to Mrs Thomas's little cottage and asked her to feed Cherub.

'I'll leave the food out for you in the shed. If you wouldn't mind feeding him twice a day? I've no idea when my cousin will be back...'

Mrs Thomas listened sympathetically. 'Don't you worry, dear, I'll look after him. He's got the cat flap so's he can get into the house, hasn't he?'

'Yes. I hate leaving him, but there's nothing I can do about it.'

'Well, she only went yesterday morning, I saw the car...and your mother and father will be back soon, I dare say?'

'I'm not sure when.'

It wasn't very satisfactory, as she explained to Cherub later, but surely someone would come home soon. Besides, she would have days off. She cheered up at the thought.

Her mother phoned in the evening. 'I thought you might be home,' she said vaguely. 'I expect you're happy to be starting at St Jules'. You see that we were right, my dear. This little job you have had hasn't made any difference at all, just a few weeks' delay. I'm sure you'll have no difficulty in catching up with the other students. Your father and I will be coming home very shortly. I can't say exactly when. The tour is such a success we may extend it. Is your cousin there?'

Araminta started to say that she wasn't, but her mother had already begun to tell her about some remarkable Celtic documents they had been examining. It took a long time to explain them and when she had finished Mrs Pomfrey said a hurried goodbye. 'I have so much to think of,' she explained. 'I'll send a card when we are coming home.'

St Jules' Hospital was old, although it had been added to, patched up and refurbished from time to time. It was a gloomy place, looming over the narrow streets surrounding it, but the entrance hall was handsome enough, with portraits of dead and gone medical men on its panelled walls and the handsome staircase sweeping up one side of it. A staircase which no one except the most senior staff were allowed to tread.

Araminta was bidden to take herself and her case to the nurses' home, reached by a rather dark tunnel at the back of the hall. There was a door at the other end and when she opened it cautiously she found herself in a small hallway with stairs ahead of her and a door marked 'Office' at one side.

It seemed sense to knock, and, bidden to go in, she opened the door.

The woman behind the small desk was middle-aged with a pale face and colourless hair, wearing a dark maroon uniform.

'Araminta Pomfrey? Come in and shut the door. I'll take you to your room presently. You can leave your outdoor things there before you go to see the Principal Nursing Officer.' She shuffled through a pile of papers.

'Here is a list of rules. You are expected to keep them while you live here. When you have completed your first year you will be allowed to live out if you wish. No smoking or drinking, no men visitors unless they visit for some good reason.'

She drew a form from a pile on the desk. 'I'll check your particulars. You are twenty-three? A good deal older than the other students. Unmarried? Parents living? British by birth?' She was ticking off the items as she read them. 'Is that your case? We will go to your room.'

They climbed the stairs, and then another flight to the floor above, and the woman opened a door half-way down a long corridor. 'You'll have your own key, of course. You will make your bed and keep your room tidy.'

The room was small and rather dark, since its window overlooked a wing of the hospital, but it was furnished nicely and the curtains and bedcover were pretty. There was a washbasin in one corner and a built-in wardrobe.

Araminta was handed a key. She asked, 'What should I call you? You are a sister?'

'I am the warden—Miss Jeff.' She looked at her watch. 'Come back to my office in ten minutes and I'll take you for your interview.'

Left alone, Araminta turned her back on the view from the window, took off her jacket and tidied her hair. She hoped she looked suitably dressed; her skirt was too long for fashion, but her blouse was crisply ironed and her shoes were well polished. She went out of the room, locked the door, put the key in her shoulder bag and found her way to Miss Jeff.

The Principal Nursing Officer's office was large, with big windows draped with velvet curtains, a carpet underfoot and a rather splendid desk. She herself was just as elegant. She was a tall woman, still good-looking, dressed in a beautifully tailored suit. She shook Araminta's hand, and told her crisply that she was fortunate that there had been an unexpected vacancy.

'Which I could have filled a dozen times, but Dr van der Breugh is an old friend and very highly thought of here in the hospital. He assured me that you had given up your place in order to cope with an emergency in his family.' She smiled. 'You are a lucky young woman to have such an important sponsor.' She studied Araminta's face. 'I hope that you will be happy here. I see no reason why you shouldn't be. You will work hard, of course, but you will make friends. You are older than the other student nurses, but I don't suppose that will make any difference.'

She nodded a friendly dismissal and Araminta went back to her room, where she unpacked and took a look at the uniform laid out on the bed. It was cotton, in blue and white stripes with a stiff belt, and there was a little badge she was to wear pinned on her chest with her name on it.

The warden had told her to go down to the canteen for her tea at four o'clock. She made her way back down the stairs and into the hospital, down more stairs into the basement. The canteen was large, with a long counter and a great many tables—most of them occupied. Araminta went to the counter, took a tray, loaded it with a plate of bread and butter and a little pot of jam, collected her tea and then stood uncertainly for a moment, not sure where she should sit. There was a variety of uniforms, so she looked for someone wearing blue and white stripes.

Someone gave her a little shove from behind. 'New, are you?'

The speaker was a big girl, wearing, to Araminta's relief, blue and white stripes, and when she nodded, she said, 'Come with me, we have to sit with our own set—the dark blue are sisters, the light blue are staff nurses. Don't go sitting with them.'

She led the way to the far end of the room to where several girls were sitting round a table. 'Here's our new girl,' she told them. 'What's your name?'

'Araminta Pomfrey.'

Several of the girls smiled, and one of them said, 'What a mouthful. Sister Tutor isn't going to like that.'

'Everyone calls me Mintie.'

'That's more like it. Sit down and have your tea. Any idea which ward you are to go to in the morning?'

'No. Whom do I ask?'

'No one. It'll be on the board outside this place; you can look presently. Have you unpacked? Supper's at eight o'clock if you're off duty. What room number are you? I'll fetch you.'

'Thank you.'

The big girl grinned. 'My name's Molly Beckett.' She waved a hand. 'And this is Jean, and that's Sue in the corner...' She named the girls one by one.

'We're all on different wards, but not all day, we have lectures and demonstrations. You'll be run off your feet on the ward, and heaven help you if Sister doesn't like you.' She got up. 'We're all on duty now, but I'm off at six o'clock; I'll see you then. Come with us and we'll look at the board.'

There was a dismayed murmur as they crowded round to look for Araminta's name.

'Baxter's,' said Molly. 'That's Sister Spicer. I don't want to frighten you, but look out for her, Mintie. She's got a tongue like a razor and if she takes a dislike to you you might as well leave.'

Araminta went back to her room, put her family

photos on the dressing table, arranged her few books on the little shelf by the bed and sat down to think. She had very little idea of what hospital life would be like and she had to admit that Sister Spicer didn't sound very promising. But she was a sensible girl and it was no use thinking about it too much until she had found her feet.

The other girls seemed very friendly, and she would be free for a few hours each day, and she could go home each week. She allowed her thoughts to wander. What was the doctor doing? she wondered. Had he missed her at all? She thought it unlikely. I must forget him, she told herself firmly. Something which should be easy, for she would have more than enough to think about.

Molly came presently and, since it wasn't time for supper, took her on a tour of the home, explaining where the different wards were and explaining the off duty. 'You'll get a couple of evenings off each week. Trouble is, you're too tired to do much. Otherwise it's a couple of hours in the morning or in the afternoon. Days off are a question of luck. We come bottom of the list, though if you've got a decent sister she'll listen if you want special days.'

The canteen was full and very noisy at suppertime. Araminta ate her corned beef and salad and the stewed apple and custard which followed it, drank a cup of strong tea and presently went to the sitting room for the more junior nursing staff. Molly had gone out for the rest of her free evening and she couldn't see any of the other girls she had met at tea. She slipped away and went to her room, had a bath and got into bed.

She told herself that it would be all right in the morning, that it was just the sudden drastic change in her lifestyle which was making her feel unhappy. She lay thinking about the doctor, telling herself that once she started her training she wouldn't let herself think of him again.

Marcus van der Breugh, dining with friends, bent an apparently attentive ear to his dinner companion while he wondered what Mintie was doing. He had told her that he didn't think she would make a good nurse and he very much feared that he was right. Possibly it was this opinion which caused his thoughts to return to her far too frequently.

CHAPTER EIGHT

LYING in bed at the end of her first day at St Jules', Araminta tried not to remember all the things which had gone wrong and reminded herself that this was the career she had wished for. Now that she had started upon it, nothing was going to deter her from completing it.

Of course, she had started off on the wrong foot. The hospital was large, and had been built in the days when long corridors and unexpected staircases were the norm. Presumably the nurses then had found nothing unusual in traipsing their length, but to Araminta, who had never encountered anything like them before, they'd spelt disaster. She had gone the wrong way, up the wrong staircase and presented herself at Sister's office only to be told that she had come to Stewart's ward; Baxter's was at the other end of the hospital and up another flight of stairs.

So she had arrived late, to encounter Sister Spicer's basilisk stare.

'You're late,' she was told. 'Why?'

'I got lost,' said Araminta.

'A ridiculous excuse. Punctuality is something I insist upon on my ward. Have you done any nursing before coming here?'

Araminta explained about the children's convalescent home, but decided against mentioning her work for the doctor.

Sister Spicer sighed. 'You will have to catch up with the other students as best you can. I suppose Sister Tutor will do what she can with you. I have no time to mollycoddle you, so you had better learn pretty fast.'

Araminta nodded her head.

'If you don't you might as well leave.'

Once upon a time Sister Spicer had probably been a nice person, reflected Araminta. Perhaps she had been crossed in love. Although she could see little to love in the cold handsome face. Poor soul, thought Araminta, and then jumped at Sister Spicer's voice. 'Well, go and find staff nurse.'

The ward was in the oldest part of the hospital, long, and lighted by a row of windows along one side, with the beds facing each other down its length occupied by women of all ages. There were two nurses making beds, who took no notice of her. At the far end Staff Nurse, identified by her light blue uniform, was bending over a trolley with another nurse beside her.

She was greeted briefly, told to go and make beds with the nurse, and thrown, as it were, to the lions.

Araminta didn't like remembering that rest of the morning. She had made beds, carried bedpans, handed round dinners and helped any number of patients in and out of bed, but never, it seemed, quite quickly enough.

'New, are yer, ducks?' one old lady had asked, with an alarming wheeze and a tendency to go purple in the face when she coughed. 'Don't you mind no one. Always in an 'urry and never no time ter tell yer anything.'

Her dinner hour had been a respite. She had sat at the table with Molly and the other students and they had been sympathetic.

'It's because you're new and no one has had the time to tell you anything. You're off at six o'clock, aren't you? And you'll come to the lectures this afternoon. Two o'clock, mind. Even Sister Spicer can't stop you.'

She had enjoyed the lectures, although she'd discovered that there was a good deal of catching up to do.

'You must borrow one of the other students' books and copy out the lectures I've already given,' Sister Tutor had said. This was an exercise which would take up several days off duty.

'But it's what I wanted,' said Araminta to herself now.

She had to admit by the end of the week that things weren't quite as she had expected them to be. According to Sister Spicer, she was lazy, slow and wasted far too much time with the patients. There was plenty of work, she had been told, without stopping to find their curlers and carry magazines to and fro,

fill water jugs and pause to admire the photos sent
from home of children and grandchildren. It was all
rather unsatisfactory, and it seemed that she would be
on Baxter's ward for three months...

She longed for her days off, and when they came
she was up early and out of the hospital, on her way
home as quickly as she could manage. She scooted
across the forecourt as fast as her legs could carry
her, watched, if she had but known, by Dr van der
Breugh, who had been called in early and was now
enjoying a cup of coffee before he went back home.

The sight of her small scurrying figure sent the
thought of her tumbling back into his head and he
frowned. He had managed for almost a whole week
to think of her only occasionally. Well, perhaps rather
more than occasionally! She would be going home
for her days off and he toyed with the idea of driving
to Hambledon to find out if she had settled in. He
squashed the idea and instead, when he encountered
one of the medical consultants on his way out of the
hospital, asked casually how the new student nurses
were shaping.

'I borrowed one of them for a few weeks and she's
been accepted late.'

'Oh, yes, I remember hearing about that. They're
quite a good bunch, but of course she has to catch
up. She's on Baxter's and Sister Spicer is a bit of a
martinet. Don't see much of the nurses, though, do
we? If I remember she was being told off for getting
the wrong patient out of bed when I saw her, some-

thing like that. Rather quiet, I thought, but Sister Spicer can take the stuffing out of anyone. Terrifies me occasionally.'

They both laughed and went on their way.

Araminta, home by mid-morning, found her cousin and Cherub to welcome her. Over coffee she made light of her first week at St Jules'.

'Have you heard from your mother?' asked Millicent. 'She phoned, but they were still busy with some new Celtic finds. She said they might not be home yet...'

'They'll be back before Christmas, though?'

'Oh, I'm sure they will! It's still October. Will you get off for the holiday?'

Araminta shook her head. 'I don't think so, I'm very junior, but of course I'll get my days off as near to Christmas Day as possible.'

'You like it? You're happy?'

Araminta assured her that she was.

The two days were soon over, but they had given her a respite, and she went back on the ward determined to make the week a better one than her first had been. It was a pity that Sister Spicer was bent on making that as difficult as possible.

Molly had told her that Sister Spicer, if she took a dislike to anyone, would go to great lengths to make life as unpleasant as possible for her. Araminta hadn't quite believed that, but now she saw that it was true. Nothing she did was quite right; she was too slow, too clumsy, too careless. She tried not to let it worry her and took comfort from the patients, who liked her. Staff Nurse was kind, too, and the two senior student nurses, although the other student nurse who was in the same set as she now was, did nothing to make life easier for her.

Melanie was a small, pretty girl, always ready with the right answers during the lectures they both attended, and, since Sister Spicer liked her, the fact that she sometimes skimped her work and was careless of the patients' comfort, went unnoticed. She was young, barely nineteen, and made it obvious that Araminta need not expect either her friendship or her help on the ward.

When once she came upon Araminta speaking to one of the house doctors she said spitefully, 'Don't you know better than to talk to the housemen? Is that why you're here? To catch yourself a husband? Just you wait and see what happens to you if Sister Spicer catches you.'

Araminta looked at her in blank astonishment. 'He was asking me the way to Outpatients; he's new.'

Melanie giggled. 'That's as good an excuse as any, I suppose, but watch out.'

Thank heavens I've got days off tomorrow, Araminta thought. Since she was off duty at six o'clock that evening, she would be able to catch a train home. She hadn't told her cousin, but she would be home by nine o'clock at the latest…

The afternoon was endless, but she went about getting patients in and out of bed, helping them, getting teas, bed pans, filling water jugs, but it was six o'clock at last and she went to the office, thankful that she could at last ask to go off duty.

Sister Spicer barley glanced up from the report she was writing.

'Have you cleaned and made up the bed in the side ward? And the locker? It may be needed. You should have done it earlier. I told Nurse Jones to tell you. Well, it's your own fault for not listening, Nurse. Go and do it now and then you may go off duty.'

'I wasn't told to do it, Sister,' Araminta said politely, 'and I am off duty at six o'clock.'

Sister Spicer did look up then. 'You'll do as you are told, Nurse—and how dare you answer back in that fashion? I shall see the Principal Nursing Sister in the morning and I shall recommend that you are entirely unsuitable for training. If I can't train you, no one else could.'

She bent her head over her desk and Araminta went back into the ward where there was a third-year nurse and Melanie, who had taken such a dislike to her. Neither of them took any notice of her as she went to the side ward and started on the bed. She very much wanted to speak her mind, but that might upset the patients and, worse, she might burst into tears. She would have her days off and when she came back *she* would go and see the Principal Nursing Officer and ask to be moved to another ward. Unheard of, but worth a try!

It was almost seven o'clock by the time she had finished readying the room and making up the bed. She went down the ward, wishing the patients a cheerful goodnight as she went, ignoring the nurses and ignoring, too, Sister's office, walking past it, out of the ward and along the corridor, then going down the wide stone staircase to the floor below and then another staircase to the ground floor.

She was trying to make up her mind as to whether it was too late to go home, or should she wait for the morning, but she was boiling with rage and misery. Nothing was turning out as she had hoped, not that that mattered now that she would never see Marcus van der Breugh again. The pain of loving him was almost physical. She swallowed the tears she must hold back until she was in her room.

'I shall probably be given the sack,' she said out loud, and jumped the last two steps, straight into the doctor's waistcoat.

'Oh,' said Araminta, as she flung her arms around as much of him as she could reach and burst into tears.

He stood patiently, holding her lightly, and not until her sobs had dwindled into hiccoughs and sniffs did he ask, 'In trouble?'

'Yes, oh, yes. You have no idea.' It seemed the most natural thing in the world to tell him, and, for the moment, the delight of finding him there just when she wanted him so badly had overridden all her good resolutions not to see him again, to forget him...

He said calmly in a voice she wouldn't have dreamt of disobeying, 'Come with me,' and he urged her across the corridor and into a room at its end.

'I can't come in here,' said Araminta. 'It's the consultants' room. I'm not allowed…'

'I'm a consultant and I'm allowing you. Sit down, Mintie, and tell me why you are so upset.'

He handed her a very white handkerchief. 'Mop up your face, stop crying and begin at the beginning.'

She stopped crying and mopped her face, but to begin at the beginning was impossible. She told him everything, muddling its sequence, making no excuses. 'And, of course, I'll be given the sack,' she finished. 'I was so rude to Sister Spicer, and anyway, she said I was no good, that I'd never make a nurse.'

She gave a sniff and blew her nose vigorously. 'It's kind of you to listen; I don't know why I had to behave like that. At least, I do, I had been looking forward to my days off, and I would have been home by now. But it's all my own fault; I'm just not cut out to be a nurse. But that doesn't matter,' she added defiantly. 'There are any number of careers these days.'

The doctor made no comment. All he said was, 'Go and wait in the nurses' sitting room until I send you a message. No, don't start asking questions. I'll explain later.'

He led her back, saw her on her way and went without haste to the Principal Nursing Officer's office. He was there for some time, using his powers of persuasion, cutting ruthlessly through rules and regulations with patience and determination which couldn't be gainsaid.

Araminta found several of her new friends in the sitting room, and it was Molly who asked, 'Not gone yet?' and then, when she saw Araminta's face, added, 'Come and sit down. We were just wondering if we'd go down to the corner and get some chips.'

Araminta said carefully, 'I meant to go home this evening, but I got held up. I—I was rude to Sister Spicer. I expect I'll be dismissed.'

She didn't feel like a grown woman, more like a disobedient schoolgirl and she despised herself for it.

Molly said bracingly, 'It can't be as bad as all that, Mintie. You'll see, when you come back from your days off you'll find it will all have blown over.'

Araminta shook her head. 'I don't think so. You see, Molly, I think Sister Spicer is probably right; I'm not very efficient, and I'm slow. I like looking after people and somehow there's never enough time. Oh, you know what I mean—someone wants a bed pan but I'm not allowed to give it because the consultant is due in five minutes—that sort of thing.'

'You've not been happy here, have you, Mintie?'

'No, to be honest I haven't. I think it will be best if I go and see the Principal Nursing Officer and tell her I'd like to leave.'

'You don't want to give it another try?' someone asked, but Araminta didn't answer because the warden had put her head round the corner.

'Nurse Pomfrey, you're to go to the consultants' room immediately.'

She went out, banging the door after her.

'Mintie, whatever is happening? Why do you have to go there?'

Araminta was at the door. 'I'll come back and tell you,' she promised.

Dr van der Breugh was standing with his vast back to the room, looking out of the window, when she knocked and went in. He turned round and gave her a thoughtful look before he spoke.

'Have you decided what you want to do?'

'Yes, I'll go and ask if I may leave. At once, if that's allowed. But I don't suppose it is.'

'And what do you intend to do?'

'It's kind of you to ask, doctor,' said Araminta, hoping that her voice wouldn't wobble. 'I shall go home and then look for the kind of job I can do. Probably they will take me back at the convalescent home.'

They wouldn't; someone had taken her place and there was no need of her services there now. But he wasn't to know that.

'I feel responsible for this unfortunate state of affairs,' said the doctor slowly, 'for it was I who persuaded you to look after the twins and then arranged for you to come here. I should have known that it would be difficult for you, having to catch up with the other students. And Sister Spicer…'

He came away from the window. 'Sit down,

Mintie, I have a suggestion to make to you. I do so
reluctantly, for you must have little faith in my powers to help you. I have a patient whose son is the
owner and headmaster of a boys' prep school at
Eastbourne. I saw her today and she told me that he
is looking urgently for a temporary assistant matron.
The previous one left unexpectedly to nurse her
mother and doesn't know when she intends to return.
I gave no thought to it until I saw you this evening.
Would you consider going there? You would need to
be interviewed, of course, but it is a job with which
you are already familiar.'

'Little boys? But how can I take the job? I am not
sure, but I expect I'd have to give some sort of notice.' She added sharply, 'Of course I have faith in
you, I'm very grateful that you should have thought
of me.'

'But if it could be arranged, you would like the
job, provided the interview was satisfactory?'

'Yes. You see, that's something I can do—little
boys and babies and girls.' She paused, then explained, 'It's not like nursing.'

'No, I realise that. So you are prepared to give it a
try? I have seen the Principal Nursing Officer. If you
go her office now you may make a request to leave.
It is already granted, but you need to go through the
motions. I will contact my patient and ask her to arrange things with her son. You should hear shortly.'

He went to the door and opened it for her. 'I will

drive you home tomorrow morning. Ten o'clock in the forecourt.'

'There is really no need…' began Araminta. 'I'm perfectly able…'

'Yes, yes, I know, but I have no time in which to argue about it. Kindly do as I ask, Mintie.'

If he had called her Miss Pomfrey in his usually coolly civil way, she would have persisted in arguing, but he had called her Mintie, in a voice kind enough to dispel any wish to argue with him. Besides, she loved him, and when you love someone, she had discovered, you wish to do everything to please them.

She said, 'Very well, doctor,' and added politely, 'Good evening.'

She went off to the office, buoyed up by the knowledge that if Marcus had said that everything was arranged, then that would be so and she had no need to worry. She knocked and, bidden to enter, received a bracing but kind lecture, a recommendation to find work more suited to her capabilities and permission to leave.

'Be sure and hand in your uniform and notify the warden. There is no need for you to see Sister Spicer.' She was offered a hand. 'I have no doubt that you will find exactly what you want, Nurse.'

So Araminta shook hands and got herself out of the office, leaving her superior thoughtful. Really, Dr van der Breugh had gone to great lengths to arrange the girl's departure. After all, he wasn't responsible for her, whatever he said. The Principal Nursing Officer wouldn't have allowed her arm to be twisted by any-one else but him; she liked him and respected him and so did everyone else at the hospital. All the same, he must be interested—such a plain little thing, too.

Araminta went back to the sitting room and half a dozen pairs of eyes fastened on her as she went in.

'Well?' asked Molly. 'Who was it? What's hap-pened? Was Sister Spicer there?'

Araminta shook her head. 'No, just me. I'm leaving in the morning…'

'But you can't. I mean, you have to give notice that you want to, and reasons.'

Araminta decided to explain. 'Well, I didn't come with the rest of you because I was asked to take on a job in an emergency. I did tell you that. But the thing is the person I worked for was Dr van der Breugh—with his nephews—and I went to look after them provided he would do his best to get me a place here as soon as possible. Well, he did, but it hasn't worked out, so now he has arranged for me to leave. The Principal Nursing Officer was very nice about it.'

There was a chorus of voices. 'What will you do? Try another hospital? Find another job?'

'Go home.'

Molly said, 'It's good of Dr van der Breugh to help you. I can quite see that he feels responsible—I mean, you obliged him in the first place, didn't you?'

'Yes. And he did warn me that he didn't think I'd be any good at nursing. Only I'd set my heart on it. I'll start again, but not just yet.'

'If you're going in the morning you'll have to pack and sort out your uniform. We'll give you a hand.'

So several of them went to Araminta's room and helped her to pack. She went in search of the warden and handed in her uniform, taking no heed of the lecture she was given by that lady, and presently they all went down to supper and then to make tea and talk about it, so that Araminta had no time at all to think or make plans. Which was a good thing, for her head was in a fine muddle. Tomorrow, she told herself, she would sit down quietly and think things out. Quite what she meant by that she didn't know.

She woke very early, her head full of her meeting with the doctor. It was wonderful that he had come into her life once more—surely for the last time. And since he had gone to so much trouble she would take this job at Eastbourne and stay there for as long as they would have her. It was work she could do, she would have some money, she could go home in the holidays and she would take care never to see Marcus again. That shouldn't be difficult, for he had never shown a wish to see more of her. She got up, and dressed, then said goodbye to her friends, and promptly at ten o'clock went down to the entrance with her case. She hadn't been particularly happy at the hospital but all the same she felt regret at leaving it.

The doctor came to meet her, took her case and put it in the boot, and settled her beside him in the car. He had wished her good morning, taken a look at her face and then decided to say nothing more for the moment. Mintie wasn't a girl to cry easily, he was sure, but he suspected that there were plenty more tears from where the last outburst had come, and it would only need a wrong word to start them off.

He drove out of the forecourt into the morning traffic.

'We will go home and have coffee, for Briskett wants to bid you goodbye. You have an appointment to see Mr Gardiner at three o'clock this afternoon. He will be at the Red Lion in Henley. Ask for him at Reception.'

He didn't ask her if she had changed her mind, and he had nothing further to say until he stopped in front of his house.

Briskett had the door open before they reached it, delighted to see her again.

'There's coffee in the small sitting room,' said Briskett, 'and I'll have your coat, Miss Pomfrey.'

They sat opposite each other by the fire, drinking Briskett's delicious coffee and eating his little vanilla biscuits, and the doctor kept up an undemanding conversation: the boys were fine, he had seen them on the previous weekend, they were all going over to Friesland for Christmas. 'They sent their love—they miss you, Mintie.'

He didn't add that he missed her, too. He must go slowly, allow her to find her feet, prove to herself that she could make a success of a job. He had admitted to himself that she had become the one thing that really mattered to him, that he loved her. He had waited a long time to find a woman to love, and now that he had he was willing to wait for her to feel the same way, something which might take time…

He drove her to Hambledon later, and once more found the house empty save for a delighted Cherub. There was another note, too, and, unlike Briskett, the doctor coolly took it from Araminta's hand when she had read it.

The cousin had gone to Kingston to shop and would be back after tea. He put the note back, ignoring her indignant look, and glanced around him. Briskett had given a faithful description of the house: pleasant, old-fashioned solid furniture and lacking a welcome.

'It's a good thing, really,' said Araminta. 'I've an awful lot to do, especially if I get this job and they want me as soon as possible.'

He rightly took this as a strong hint that he should go. He would have liked to have taken her somewhere for a meal but she would have refused. When she thanked him for the lift and his help in getting her another job, he made a noncommittal reply, evincing no wish to see her again, but wishing her a happy future. And in a month or two he would contrive to see her again…

Araminta, wishing him goodbye and not knowing that, felt as though her heart would break—hearts never did, of course, but it was no longer a meaningless nonsense.

But there was little time to indulge in unhappiness. In three hours' time she would have to be at the Red Lion in Henley, and in the meantime there was a lot to do.

There had been no time to have second thoughts; that evening, washing and ironing, sorting out what clothes she would take with her while she listened to her cousin's chatter, Araminta wondered if she had been too hasty.

Mr Gardiner had been no time-waster. He was a man of early middle age, quiet and taciturn, asking her sensible questions and expecting sensible answers. His need for an assistant matron was urgent, with upwards of fifty little boys and Matron run off her feet. He'd read her credentials, then voiced the opinion that they seemed satisfactory.

'In any case,' he told her, 'my mother tells me that Dr van der Breugh is a man of integrity and highly respected. He gave you a most satisfactory reference. Now, as to conditions and salary…'

He dealt with these quite swiftly and asked, 'Are you prepared to come? As soon as possible?' He smiled suddenly. 'Could you manage tomorrow?'

The sooner she had something to occupy her thoughts the better, reflected Araminta. She agreed to start on the following day. 'In the late afternoon? Would that do? There are several things I must see to…'

'Of course, we'll expect you around teatime. Take

a taxi from the station and put it down to expenses. I don't suppose you have a uniform? I'll get Matron to find something.'

He had given her tea and she had come back home to find her cousin returned. A good thing, for she'd offered to cook them a meal while Araminta began on her packing. She'd phoned her mother later to tell her that she had left the hospital and was taking up a job as an assistant school matron.

'What a good idea,' observed her parent comfortably. 'You liked the convalescent home, didn't you? A pity you couldn't have stayed with Dr van der Breugh's nephews, for it seems to me, my love, that you are cut out to be a homebody. I'm sure you will be very happy at Eastbourne.

'We shall be home very shortly and we must make plans for Christmas. We still have a good deal of research to do and the publishers are anxious for us to have our book ready by the spring, but we shall be home soon, although we may need to make a trip to Cornwall—there have been some interesting discoveries made near Bodmin.'

Araminta was sorry to leave Cherub once again. It was fortunate that he was a self-sufficient cat, content as long as he was fed and could get in and out of the house. Araminta, on her way to Eastbourne the next day, wondered if it would be possible for her to have him with her at the school. There was a flatlet, Mr Gardiner had told her, and Cherub would be happy in her company. She would wait until she had been there for a time and then see what could be done. It depended very much on the matron she would be working with. Araminta, speculating about her, decided that no one could be worse than Sister Spicer...

The school was close to the sea front, a large rambling place surrounded by a high brick wall, but the grounds around it were ample; there were tennis courts and a covered swimming pool and a cricket pitch. And the house looked welcoming.

She was admitted by a friendly girl who took her straight to Mr Gardiner's office. He got up to shake hands, expressed pleasure at her arrival and suggested that she might like to go straight to Matron.

'I'll take you up and leave you to get acquainted. The boys will be at supper very shortly, and then they have half an hour's recreation before bed. Perhaps you could work alongside Matron for a while this evening and get some idea of the work?'

Matron had a sitting room and a bedroom on the first floor next to the sick bay. She was a youngish woman with a round, cheerful face and welcomed Araminta warmly. Over a pot of tea she expressed her relief at getting help.

'It's a good job here,' she observed. 'The Gardiners are very kind and considerate, but it does need two of us. You like small boys? Mr Gardiner told me that you had worked with them.'

She took Araminta along to her room presently, at the other end of the house but on the same floor. It was quite large, with a shower room leading from it, an electric fire, a gas ring and a kettle. It was comfortably furnished and on the bed there was an assortment of blue and white striped dresses.

'I've done the best I could,' said Matron. 'See if any of them fit—the best of them can be altered.' She hesitated. 'Mr Gardiner always calls me Matron—but the name's Pagett, Norma. I should call you Matron as well, when the boys are around, but...' She paused enquiringly.

'Would you call me Mintie? It's Araminta, really, but almost no one calls me that. Do I call you Miss Pagett?'

'Heavens no, call me Norma. I'm sure we shall get on well together.'

Norma went back to her room and left Araminta to try on the dresses. One or two were a tolerable fit, so she changed, unpacked her few things and went back to Norma's room.

There was just time to be given a brief resumé of her work before the boys' suppertime, and presently, presiding over a table of small boys gobbling their suppers, Araminta felt a surge of content. She wasn't happy, but it seemed that she had found the right job at last—and who could be miserable with all these little boys talking and shouting, pushing and shoving and then turning into pious little angels when Mr Gardiner said grace at the end of the meal?

Later that evening, sitting in her dressing gown, drinking cocoa in Norma's room, Araminta reminded herself that this was exactly what she had wanted. She would never be a career girl, but she hoped there would be a secure and pleasant future ahead for her.

Hard on this uplifting thought came another one. She didn't want security and life could be as unpleasant as it liked, if only she could see Marcus again.

The next few days gave her no chance to indulge in self-pity. Accustomed as she was to the care of small children, she still found the day's workload heavy. Norma was well organised, being a trained children's nurse, and efficient. She was kind and patient, too, and the boys liked her. They liked Araminta, too, and once she had learned her day's routine, and her way round the school, she found that life could be pleasant enough even if busy—provided, of course, that she didn't allow herself to think about Marcus.

The following weekend was an exeat, and the boys would have Saturday, Sunday and Monday to go home, save for a handful whose parents were abroad.

'We will split the weekend between us,' Norma told her, 'I'll have Friday evening—you can manage, can't you?—and come back on Sunday at midday. You can have the rest of Sunday and Monday, only be back in the evening, won't you? The boys will come back after tea. Mr Gardiner doesn't mind how we arrange things as long as one of us is here to keep an eye on the boys who are staying—there aren't many; all but half a dozen have family or friends to whom they go.'

'I don't mind if I don't go home,' said Araminta. 'I've only just got here...'

'Nice of you, but fair's fair, and you'll be glad of a couple of days away. This is always a busy term—Christmas and the school play and parents coming and the boys getting excited.'

Marcus van der Breugh, busy man though he was, still found time to phone Mrs Gardiner senior. 'A happy coincidence,' he told her, 'that you should have mentioned your son's urgent need for help. I am sure that Miss Pomfrey will be suitable for the work.'

Mrs Gardiner, with time on her hands, was only too glad to chat.

'I heard from him yesterday evening. He is very satisfied. She seems a nice girl—the boys like her and the matron likes her. So important that these people should get on well together, don't you agree? And, of course, she is fortunate in that it is an exeat at the weekend and she will be free for part of the time to go home. She and Matron will share the days between them, of course; someone has to be there for the boys who stay at the school.' She gave a satisfied laugh. 'I feel we must congratulate ourselves on arranging things so successfully.'

The doctor, making suitable replies when it seemed necessary, was already making plans.

Araminta was surprised to get a letter the next morning; her parents were still away and the writing on the envelope wasn't her cousin's. She opened it slowly; her first delighted thought that it was from the doctor was instantly squashed. The writing was a woman's; his writing was almost unreadable.

It was from Lucy Ingram. She had asked her brother where Araminta was, she wrote, and he had given her the school's address. Could Araminta come and stay for a day or two when she was next free? The boys were so anxious to see her again. 'It's an exeat next weekend and I dare say all the schools are the same. So if you are free, do let us know. I'll drive over and fetch you. Do come if you can; it will be just us. Will you give me a ring?'

Araminta phoned that evening. It would be nice to see Peter and Paul again, and perhaps hear something of Marcus from his sister. She accepted with pleasure but wondered if it was worth Mrs Ingram's drive. 'It's only a day and a half,' she pointed out, 'and it's quite a long way.'

'The M4, M25, and a straight run down to Eastbourne. I'll be there on Sunday at noon. And we shall love to see you again.'

The school seemed very empty once most of the boys had gone and Norma had got into her elderly car and driven away. There were eight boys left, and with Mr Gardiner's permission Araminta had planned one or two treats for the next day. The pier was still open and some of the amusements—the slot machines, the games which never yielded up a prize, the fortune-teller—were still there.

After their midday dinner she marshalled her little flock and, armed with a pocket full of tenpenny pieces which she handed out amongst them, she let them try everything and then trotted them along the esplanade and into the town, where they had tea at one of the smartest cafés.

Mr Gardiner had told her to give them a good time, that she would be reimbursed, so they ate an enormous tea and, content with their outing, walked back through the dusk to the school. Since it was a holiday they were allowed to stay up for an hour and watch television after their supper. Araminta, going from bed to bed wishing them goodnight, was almost as tired as they were.

She put everything ready for the morning before she went to bed, praying that Norma would be as good as her word and return punctually.

She did. Araminta, back from church with the boys and Mr Gardiner and his wife, wished everyone a hurried goodbye and went out of the school gate to find Mrs Ingram waiting there.

'You've not been waiting long?' she asked breathlessly. 'It's been a bit of a scramble.'

'Five minutes. How nice to see you again, Mintie. I thought we'd stop for lunch on the way; we'll be home before three o'clock and then we'll have an early tea with the boys. They can't wait to see you again.'

'It's very kind of you to invite me. I—I didn't expect to see you or the boys again.'

'You like this new job?' Mrs Ingram was driving fast along the almost empty road.

'Yes, very much. I've only been here for a week. I started nursing, but I wasn't any good at it. Dr van der Breugh happened to see me at the hospital and arranged for me to give up training, and he happened to know of this school. He's been very kind.'

Mrs Ingram shot her a quick look. 'Yes, he is. Far too busy, too. We don't see enough of him, so thank heaven for the phone. Now, tell me, what exactly do you do?'

The drive seemed shorter than it was; they found plenty to talk about, and stopped for a snack meal at a service station. The time passed pleasantly and, true to her word, Mrs Ingram stopped the car at her home just before three o'clock.

CHAPTER NINE

PETER and Paul fell upon her with a rapturous welcome. They had missed her, they chorused, and did she still remember the Dutch they had taught her when they were in Holland? And did she remember that lovely toy shop? And why did she have to live so far away? And was she to stay for a long, long time? For they had, assured Peter, an awful lot to tell her. But first she must go into the garden and see the goldfish...

They had a splendid tea presently, and then everyone sat around the table and played Snakes and Ladders, Ludo and the Racing Game, relics from Mr Ingram's childhood. Then it was time for supper, and nothing would do but that Araminta should go upstairs when they were in bed and tell them a story.

'You always did in Uncle Marcus's house,' they reminded her.

The day was nicely rounded off by dinner with the Ingrams and an hour or so round the drawing room fire talking about everything under the sun, except Marcus.

It was still dark when she awoke in the pretty bedroom.

'It's a bit early,' said Peter as the pair of them got

onto her bed and pulled the eiderdown around them, 'but you've got to go again at tea time, haven't you? So we thought you might like to wake up so's we can talk.'

The day went too quickly. They didn't go out, for the weather had turned nasty—a damp, misty, chilly November day—but there had been plenty to do indoors. It was mid-afternoon when Mr Ingram took the boys into the garden to make sure that the goldfish were alive and waiting for their food, leaving Mrs Ingram and Araminta sitting in the drawing room, talking idly.

They were discussing clothes. 'It must be delightful—' began Araminta, and stopped speaking as the door opened and the doctor came in.

He nodded, smiling, at his sister, and said, 'Hello, Mintie.'

Nothing could have prevented her glorious smile at the sight of him. He noted it with deep satisfaction and watched her pale cheeks suddenly pinken.

'Good afternoon, Doctor,' said Araminta, replacing the smile with what she hoped was mild interest, bending to examine one of her shoes.

Mrs Ingram got up to kiss him. 'Marcus, how very punctual you are. We're about to have tea. Such a pity that Araminta has to go back this evening.'

The doctor glanced at his watch. 'You have to be back to get the boys settled in again?' he asked Araminta. 'If we leave around four o'clock that should get you there in good time.'

Araminta looked at Mrs Ingram, who said airily, 'Oh, you won't mind if Marcus drives you back, will you, Araminta? After all, you do know each other, and you'll have plenty to talk about.'

'But it's miles out of your way...?'

Araminta, filled with delight at the thought of several hours in Marcus's company, nonetheless felt it her duty to protest.

'I am interested to hear how you are getting on at the school,' he observed blandly. 'I feel sure that there will be no chance to discuss that once the boys have come indoors.'

Which was true enough. They swarmed over their uncle and grown-up conversation of any kind was at a minimum. Tea was eaten at the table: plates of thinly cut bread and butter, crumpets, toasted tea-cakes, a sponge cake and a chocolate cake.

'The boys chose what we should have for tea—all the things you like most, Araminta,' said Mrs Ingram. 'And, I suspect, all the things they like most, too! We always have an old-fashioned tea with them. I can't say I enjoy milkless tea and one biscuit at four o'clock.'

She glanced at her brother. 'Did you have time for lunch, Marcus?'

'Oh, yes. It's Briskett's day off, but he leaves me something.' He sounded vague. But there was nothing vague about his manner when presently he said that they must leave if Araminta needed to be back at the school by six o'clock. She fetched her overnight bag

and got into her coat, then made her farewells—
lengthy ones when it came to the boys, who didn't
want her to go.

'Araminta must come and see us all again soon,'
said Mr Ingram. 'She gets holidays just like you do.'

A remark which served to cheer up the boys so that
she and Marcus left followed by a cheerful chorus of
goodbyes.

Beyond asking her if she were comfortable, the
doctor had nothing to say. It wasn't until they were
on the M4, travelling fast through the early dusk, that
he began a desultory conversation about nothing in
particular. He was intent on putting Araminta at her
ease, for she was sitting stiff as a poker beside him,
giving him the strong impression that given the opportunity she would jump out of the car.

She had said very little to him at his sister's house,
something which no one but himself had noticed, and
now she was behaving as though he were a stranger.
Driving to Oxford that afternoon, he had decided to
ask her to marry him, but now he could see that that
was something he must not do. For some reason she
was keeping him at arm's length, and yet at St Jules'
she had flung those arms around him with every appearance of relief and delight at seeing him. She
seemed happy enough at the school. Perhaps she was
trying to make it plain that she resented his reap-
pearance now that she had settled into a job that she
liked.

They reached the M25 and he was relieved to see

that her small stern profile had resolved itself into her usual habitual expression of serenity. He waited until they had left the motorway, going south now towards Eastbourne.

'You are happy at the school?' he asked casually. 'You feel that you can settle there, if permanent job should be offered, or would you prefer to use it as a stop-gap? You can always enrol at another hospital, you know.'

'No. That was a mistake. I hope that I can stay at the school. Matron is thinking of leaving next year; there's always the chance that I might get her job. I would be very happy there for the rest of my life.'

She spoke defiantly, expecting him to disagree about that, but all he did was grunt in what she supposed was agreement, which should have pleased her but left her illogically disappointed.

Presently he said, 'You feel that you have found your niche in life?' He shot past a slow-moving car. 'Have you no wish to marry? Have a home of your own, a husband and children?'

It was on the tip of her tongue to tell him that was exactly what she wished, but what would be the point of wishing? Where was she to find a home and a husband and children? And anyway, the only husband she wanted was beside her, although he might just as well have been on the moon.

She wasn't going to answer that; instead she asked, 'And you, doctor, don't you wish for a wife and children?'

'Indeed I do. What is more, I hope to have both in due course.'

Not Christina, hoped Araminta, he would be unhappy. She said, at her most Miss Pomfrey-ish, 'That will be nice.'

A silly answer, but what else was there to say? She tried to think of a suitable remark which might encourage him to tell her more, but her mind was blank. Only her treacherous tongue took matters into its own hands.

'Is she pretty?' asked Araminta, and went scarlet with shame, thankful that it was too dark for him to see her face.

The doctor managed not to smile. He said in a matter-of-fact way, as though there was nothing unusual in her question, 'I think she is the loveliest girl in the world.'

To make amends, Araminta said, 'I hope you will be very happy.'

'Oh, I am quite certain of that. Paul and Peter are looking very fit, don't you agree?'

Such a pointed change in the conversation couldn't be ignored. She was aware of being snubbed and her reply was uttered in extreme politeness with waspish undertones. It seemed the right moment to introduce that safest of topics, the weather.

She spun it out, making suitable comments at intervals, and the doctor, making equally suitable answers in a casual fashion, was well content. True, his Araminta had shown no sign of love, even liking for him, but she was very much on her guard and anxious to impress him with her plans for her solitary future.

But he had seen her gloved hands clenched together on her lap and the droop of her shoulders. She wasn't happy, despite her assurances. He wished very much to tell her that he loved her, but it was only too obvious that she was holding him at arm's length. Well, he could wait. In a week or so he would find a reason to meet her again…

They were in the outskirts of Eastbourne and he glanced at the clock on the dashboard. 'Ten minutes to six. Do you go on duty straight away?'

'I expect so. There'll be the unpacking to do, and the boys will want their supper.'

He stopped the car by the school entrance and she undid her seat belt. 'Thank you for bringing me back; I have so enjoyed my weekend. Don't get out—you must be anxious to get home.'

He took no notice of that but got out, opened her door, got her case from the boot and walked her to the door.

She held out a hand. 'Goodbye, Dr van der Breugh. I hope you have a lovely time at Christmas.'

He didn't speak. He put her case down in the vestibule and bent and kissed her, slowly and gently. And only by a great effort was she able to keep her arms from flinging themselves round him. He got back into his car then, and drove away, and she stood, a prey to a great many thoughts and feelings, oblivious of the small boys trooping to and fro in the hall behind her.

Their small voices, piping greetings, brought her to her senses and back into the busy world of the school. It was only that night in bed that she had the time to go over those last few moments.

Had he meant to kiss her like that? she wondered. Or was it a kind of goodbye kiss? After all, if he intended to marry, he would have no further interest in her, and any interest he might have had had been more or less thrust upon him.

She was glad that she had been so positive about the future she had planned for herself. She must have convinced him that she had no interest in getting married. There were hundreds of girls who had made independent lives for themselves and there was no reason why she shouldn't be one of them.

No one would mind. Her mother and father would want her to be happy, but it wouldn't worry them if she didn't marry.

She was too tired to cry and tomorrow morning was only a few hours away. She went into an uneasy sleep and dreamed of Marcus.

With Christmas only weeks away there was a good deal of extra activity at the school: the play, the school concert, the older boys carol-singing in the town, and all of the boys making Christmas presents. Model aeroplanes, boats, spacecraft were all in the process of being glued, nailed and painted, destined for brothers and sisters at home. Cards were designed and painted, drawings framed for admiring mothers and fathers, calendars cut out and suitably ornamented for devoted grannies, and, as well as all this, there were lessons as usual.

Araminta, racing round making beds, looking for small lost garments, helping to write letters home, helping with the presents and making suitable costumes for the play, and that on top of her usual chores, had no time to think about her own life. Only at last when she had her free day did she take time to think about the future.

She didn't go home; her parents would be coming back during the following week and she would go then. She wrapped up warmly and walked briskly along the promenade, oblivious of the wind and the rain.

It seemed obvious to her that she wouldn't see Marcus again. It must have been pure chance which led him to visit his sister while she was staying there. Indeed, it was always pure chance when they met. He had had no choice but to offer to drive her back to Eastbourne.

'I must forget him,' said Araminta, shouting it into the wind.

She turned her back on that same wind presently and got blown back the way she had come. In the town she found a small, cosy restaurant and had a meal, then spent the afternoon shopping. Dull items like toothpaste, hand cream and a new comb, some

of the ginger nuts Norma liked with her evening cocoa and coloured wrapping paper for some of the
boys whose gifts were finished and ready to pack up.

She had an extravagant tea presently, prolonging it
as long as possible by making a list of the Christmas
presents she must buy. Then, since the shops were
still open, she spent a long time choosing cards, but
finally that was done and there was nothing for her
to do but go back to the school.

The cinema was showing a horror film, which
didn't appeal, and besides, she didn't like the idea of
going alone. The theatre was shut prior to opening
with the yearly pantomime.

She bought a packet of sandwiches and went back
to her room; she would make tea on her gas ring and
eat her sandwiches and read the paperbacks she had
chosen. She had enjoyed her day, she assured herself.
All the same she was glad when it was morning and
she could plunge headfirst into the ordered chaos of
little boys.

At the end of another week she went home for the
day. It was a tedious journey, travelling to London by
train and then on to Henley where her father met her
with the car. He was glad to see her, observed that
she looked very well and plunged into an account of
his and her mother's tour. It had been an undoubted
success, he told her, and they would be returning at
a future date. The details of their trip lasted until they
reached the house, where her mother was waiting for
them.

'You look very well, my dear,' she told Araminta. 'This little job is obviously exactly right for you. Did your father tell you about our success? I'm sure he must have left out a good deal...'

Even if Araminta had wanted to talk to her mother there was no chance; they loved her, but she couldn't compete against the Celts. After all, they had been involved with them long before she was born. Her unexpected late arrival must have interfered with their deep interest in Celtic lore, but only for a short time. Nannies, governesses and school had made her independent at an early age and she had accepted that.

She listened now, made suitable comments and, since her cousin had gone to Henley to the dentist, cooked lunch. It was only later, while they were having tea, that her mother asked, 'You enjoyed your stay with those little boys? Dr Jenkell has told us what a charming man their uncle is. You were well treated?'

'Oh, yes, Mother, and the boys were delightful children. We got on well together and I liked Holland. Utrecht is a lovely old city...'

'I dare say it is. A pity you had no time to explore the *hunebedden* in Drenthe and the *terps* in Friesland; so clever of those primitive people to build their villages on mounds of earth. Your father and I must find the time to visit them. I'm sure something can be arranged; he knows several people at Groningen University.'

Araminta poured second cups and passed the cake. 'You will be home for Christmas?'

'Yes, yes, of course we shall. We are going to Southern Ireland next week, for your father has been invited to give a short lecture tour and there are several places I wish to see—verifying facts before we revise the book. It will be published next year, I hope…'

'I get almost three weeks' holiday,' said Araminta.

Her mother said vaguely, 'Oh, that's nice, dear. You'll come home, of course?'

'Yes.' Araminta looked at her cousin. 'I could take over for a week or so if you wanted to go away.'

An offer which was accepted without hesitation.

Back at school, activities became feverish; the play was to be presented to an audience of parents who could get there, friends who lived locally and the school staff. So costumes had to have last-minute fittings, boys who suddenly lost their nerve had to be encouraged, the school hall had to be suitably decorated, and refreshments dealt with. Everyone was busy and Araminta told herself each night when she went to bed that with no leisure to brood she would soon forget Marcus; he would become a dim figure in her past.

She shut her eyes, willed herself to sleep and there he was, his face behind her lids, every well-remembered line of it; the tiny crow's feet round his eyes when he smiled, the little frown mark where he perched his spectacles, the haughty nose, the thin, firm mouth, the lines when he was tired…

It will take time, thought Araminta, shaking up her pillows, and she tried to ignore the thought that it would take the rest of her life and beyond.

It wasn't only the school play. The carol-singers had to be rounded up and rehearsed, and someone had discovered that she could play the piano, so that each evening for half an hour she played carols, not always correctly but with feeling, sometimes joining in the singing.

The school concert would be held on the very last day, so that parents coming to collect their small sons could applaud their skills. There were to be recitations, duets on the piano, and a shaky rendering of 'Silent Night' by a boy who was learning the violin and a promising pianist. It was a pity that the two boys didn't get on well and rehearsals were often brought to a sudden end while they squabbled.

But it was a happy time for them all and Araminta, sitting up in bed long after she should have been asleep, fashioning suitable costumes for the Three Kings, to be sung by three of the older boys, although she was unhappy, was learning to live with her unhappiness. The answer was work; to be occupied for as many hours as there was daylight and longer than that so that she was too tired to think when she went to bed.

She didn't go home on her next day off, but spent the day buying Christmas presents and writing cards. Her parents had never celebrated Christmas in the traditional way; they exchanged presents and Araminta made Christmas puddings and mince pies, but there was never a tree or decorations in the house. This year, now that she had money to spend, she determined to make it a festive occasion. So she shopped for baubles for the tree, and tinsel, candles in pretty holders, crackers in pretty wrappings.

There was a tree set up in the Assembly Hall at school, too, and the boys were allowed to help decorate it. The nearer the end of term came the more feverish became the activity. End of term examinations were taken, reports made out and the boys' clothes inspected ready for packing. After the concert there would be a prize giving, and then the boys would go home. Araminta was to stay for another day, helping Norma leave the dormitories and recreation rooms tidy, before they, too, would go home.

Before the end of term the Gardiners gave a small party for the staff. Araminta had met them all, of course, but saw very little of them socially. She changed into a pretty dress and went with Norma to drink sherry and nibble savoury biscuits and exchange small talk with the form masters, the little lady who taught music and the French girl who taught French. Mr Gardiner was kind, asking her if she enjoyed her work, wanting to know what she was doing for Christmas, and Mrs Gardiner admired her dress.

The last day came, a round of concert, prize-giving and seeing the boys all safely away. Even those few whose parents were abroad were going to stay with friends or relatives, so that by suppertime the school was empty of boys and several of the staff.

Araminta and Norma began on the task of stripping beds, making sure that the cupboards and lockers were empty, checking the medicine chest and the linen cupboard, and then they spent the next morning sorting bed linen, counting blankets and making sure that everything was just so. They would return two days before the boys to make up beds and get things shipshape.

Norma was ready to leave after lunch. 'I'll go and see Mr Gardiner,' she told Araminta, 'and then go straight out to the car. So I'll say goodbye and a Happy Christmas now. You'll catch the train later? Have a lovely Christmas.'

Araminta finished her own packing, took her case and the bag packed with presents down to the hall and went in search of Mr Gardiner.

He was in his study, sitting at his desk, and looked up as she went in.

'Ah, Miss Pomfrey, you have come to say goodbye. You have done very well and I am more than pleased with you; you certainly helped us through a dodgy period.' He leaned back in his chair and gave her a kind smile.

'I am only sorry that we cannot offer you a permanent position here; I have heard from our assistant matron, who tells me that her mother has died and she has begged for her job back again. She has been with us for a number of years and, given that your position was temporary, I feel it only fair to offer her the post again. I am sure you will have no difficulty in finding another post; I shall be only too glad to recommend you. There is always a shortage of school matrons, you know.'

Araminta didn't say anything; she was dumb with disappointment and surprise, her future crumbling before her eyes just as she had felt sure that she had found security at last. She had really convinced herself that the previous Matron would not return. Mr Gardiner coughed. 'We are really sorry,' he added, 'but I'm sure you will understand.'

She nodded. 'Yes, of course, Mr Gardiner...'

He looked relieved. 'The post was brought to me a short while ago; there is a letter for you.' He handed her an envelope and stood up, offering a hand. 'Your train goes shortly? Stay here as long as you wish. I'm sure they will give you a cup of tea if you would like that before you go.'

'Thank you, there is a taxi coming for me.'

She shook hands and smiled, although smiling was very difficult, and went quickly out of the room.

In the hall she sat down and opened her letter. It was from her mother.

Araminta would understand, she felt sure, that she and her father had been offered a marvellous opportunity to go to Italy, where there had been the most interesting finds. Splendid material for the book, wrote her mother, and an honour for her father. They would return as soon as they could—some time in the

New Year. 'You will have your cousin for company,' finished her mother, 'and I'm sure you will be glad of a quiet period.'

Araminta read the letter twice, because she simply hadn't believed it the first time, but it was true, written clearly in ink in her mother's flowing hand. She folded the letter carefully, then crossed the hall to the telephone and dialled her home number.

Her cousin answered. 'I've had a letter from mother,' began Araminta. 'It was a bit of a surprise. I'm catching the five o'clock train from here, so I'll be home for supper...'

There was silence for a few minutes. 'Araminta, I won't be here. Didn't your mother tell you? No, of course, she would have forgotten. I'm on the point of leaving—Great Aunt Kate is ill and I'm going to Bristol to nurse her. I've left food in the fridge and Cherub is being looked after until you come. I'm sorry, dear. Your mother and father left in a hurry and I don't suppose they thought... Could you not stay with friends? I'll come back just as soon as I can.'

Araminta found her voice; it didn't sound quite like hers, but she forced it to sound cheerful. 'Don't worry, I'll be quite glad of a quiet time after rushing round here. I'll look up some friends in the village. I'm sorry you won't be at home, and I hope Christmas won't be too busy for you.'

She must end on a bright note. 'My taxi's just arrived and I mustn't keep it waiting. Let me know how you get on. I'll be at home for a couple of weeks, and you may be back by then.' She added, 'Happy Christmas,' with false brightness.

The taxi had arrived. It was too early for the train but she had planned to leave her luggage at the station and have tea in the town. Now all she wanted was to go somewhere and sit as far away from people as possible. She didn't want to think, not yet. First she must come to terms with disappointment.

She got into the taxi. 'Will you drive me along the promenade? I'll tell you where I want to be put down.'

It was dusk already, and cold. The promenade was bare of people and only a handful of cars were on it. Away from the main street it was quiet, only the sound of the sea and the wind whistling down a side street. She asked the driver to stop and got out, took her case and bag, then paid him, assuring him that this was where she wished to be, and watched him drive away.

She crossed the road to a shelter facing the sea. It was an old-fashioned edifice, with its benches sheltered from the wind and the rain by a roof and glassed-in walls. She put her luggage down and sat down in one corner facing the sea. It was cold, but she hadn't noticed that; she was arranging her thoughts in some kind of order. Just for a short time she allowed disappointment to engulf her, a disappointment all the more bitter because she hadn't really expected it—nor would it have been as bad if she had gone home to a loving family, waiting to welcome her.

'Wallowing in self-pity will do you no good, my girl,' said Araminta loudly. 'I must weigh the pros and cons.'

She ticked them off on her gloved fingers. 'I have some money, I have a home to go to, I can get another job after Christmas, Mother and Father…' She faltered. 'And there is Cherub waiting for me.'

Those were the pros, and for the moment she refused to think of anything else. But presently she had to, for she couldn't sit there for the rest of the evening and all night. The idea of going home to an empty house was something she couldn't face for the moment, although she could see that there was nothing else that she could do. She had friends in the village, but she had lost contact with them; her parents were liked and respected, but hardly neighbourly. There was no one to whom she could go and beg to stay with, especially at Christmas, when everyone had family and friends staying.

The tears she had been swallowing back crawled slowly down her cheeks.

The doctor was well aware that school had broken up, and upon which day Araminta would be going home for the holidays; old Mrs Gardiner had been delighted to have another little gossip when she had visited him at his consulting rooms. She had even volunteered the information that the teaching staff and the matrons stayed at the school for an extra day in order to leave everything tidy. And she had added, 'Miriam—my daughter-in-law—told me that the matrons stay until the late afternoon. They have a good deal to see to, but she is always glad when they have gone and the school is empty. I shall be going there for Christmas, of course.'

It took a good deal of planning, but by dint of working early and late the doctor achieved his object. By two o'clock he was driving away from St Jules', on his way to Eastbourne.

Araminta had left the school ten minutes before he stopped before its gates.

'Gone to catch the five o'clock train,' the maid who answered his ring told him. 'I said she was too early, but she was going to have tea somewhere first.'

The doctor thanked her with a civility which quite belied his feelings, then drove into the town, parked the car and began his search. The station first, and then every tea room, café, restaurant and snack bar. Araminta had disappeared into thin air in the space of half an hour or so.

The doctor went back to the station. He was tired, worried and angry, but nothing of his feelings showed on his face. He searched the station again, enquired at the ticket office, questioned the porters and went back to the entrance. There was a row of taxis lined up, waiting for the next train from London, and he went from one to the other, making his enquiries in a calm unhurried manner.

The third cabby, lolling beside his cab, took a cigarette out of his mouth to answer him.

'Young lady? With a case? Booked to go to the station, but changed her mind. Looking for her, are you?'

'Yes, will you tell me where you took her?'

'Well, now, I could do that, but I don't know who you are, do I?'

'You're quite right to ask. My name is van der Breugh. I'm a doctor. The young lady's name is Miss Araminta Pomfrey. She is my future wife. If you will take me to her, you could perhaps wait while we talk and then bring us back here. My car is in the car park.' He smiled. 'If you wish you may accompany me when I meet her.'

The man stared at him. 'I'll take you and I'll wait.'

Araminta, lost in sad thoughts, didn't hear the taxi, and didn't hear the doctor's footsteps. Only when he said quietly, 'Hello, Mintie,' did she look up, her mouth open and her eyes wide. All she said was, 'Oh.'

It was apparently enough for the doctor. He picked up her case and the plastic bag and said in a brisk voice, 'It's rather chilly here. We'll go somewhere and have a cup of tea.'

'No,' said Araminta, then added, 'I'm going home.'

'Well, of course you are. Come along, the taxi's waiting.'

The utter surprise of seeing him had addled her

wits. She crossed the road and got into the taxi, and when the cabby asked, 'OK, miss?' she managed to give him a shaky smile. She was cold, her head felt empty, and it was too much trouble to think for the moment. She sat quietly beside Marcus until the taxi stopped before a tea room, its lighted windows welcoming in the dark evening. She stood quietly while the doctor paid the cabby, picked up her luggage, opened the tea room door and sat her down at a table.

The place was half full, for it was barely five o'clock, and it was warm and cosy with elderly waitresses carrying loaded trays. The doctor gave his order, took off his overcoat, then leaned across and unbuttoned her jacket, and in those few minutes Araminta had pulled herself together.

'I do not know why you have brought me here,' she said frostily.

'I was hoping that you would tell me,' said Marcus mildly. 'The school has broken up for the holidays, everyone has gone home but you are still here, sitting in a shelter on the promenade with your luggage. Why are you not at home, Mintie?'

His voice would have melted the Elgin Marbles, and Araminta was flesh and blood.

She said gruffly, 'I've been made redundant—the other girl is coming back. I thought I'd just stay here for a day or two.'

'And why would you wish to do that?' His voice was very quiet—a voice to calm a frightened child…

'Well,' began Araminta, 'there's really no need for

me to go home. Mother and father have gone to Italy—the Celts, you know—and my cousin has had to go to an aunt who is ill. There's only Cherub…'

He perceived that Cherub was the only close tie she had with her home. He said nothing, but his silence was comforting, so that she went on, pot-valiant, 'I shall have no trouble in getting another job. I'm well qualified…'

A gross exaggeration, this, in a world of diploma holders and possessors of degrees, but she wouldn't admit that, not even to herself, and certainly not to him.

The doctor remained silent, watching her from under his lids while she drank her tea.

'Well, I must be going.' She had never been so unhappy in her life, but she must get away before she burst into tears. 'I cannot think why I have wasted my time here. I suppose you were just curious?'

'Yes.' He had spent a good deal of time and trouble looking for her, but he found himself smiling. He said in his quiet voice, 'Will you marry me, Mintie?' and watched the colour creep into her pale face as she stared at him across the table. 'I fell in love with you the moment I set eyes on you, although I wasn't aware of that at the time. Now I love you so deeply I find that I cannot live without you, my darling.'

Araminta took a minute to understand this. 'Me? You love me? But I thought you didn't like me—only you always seemed to be there when I had got into a mess. You—you ignored me.'

'I did not know what else to do. I am years older than you; you might have met a younger man.' He smiled suddenly and she felt a warm tide of love sweep over her. 'Besides, you were always Miss Pomfrey, holding me at arm's length, so I have waited patiently, hoping that you might learn to love me. But now I can wait no longer.' He added, 'If you want me to go away, I will, Mintie.'

Her voice came out in a terrified squeak. 'Go away? Don't go—oh, please, don't go. I couldn't bear it, and I want to marry you more than anything else in the world.'

The doctor glanced around him, for those sitting near their table were showing signs of interest. He laid money on the table, got into his overcoat, buttoned her jacket and said, 'Let us leave…'

'Why?' asked Araminta, awash with happiness.

'I want to kiss you.'

They went outside into the dark afternoon, into their own private heaven. The narrow street was almost empty—there were only two women laden with shopping bags, an old man with his dog, and a posse of carol-singers about to start up. Neither the doctor nor Araminta noticed them. He wrapped his great arms round her and held her close, and as the first rousing verse of 'Good King Wenceslas' rang out, he kissed her.

MILLS & BOON®

Makes any time special™

Mills & Boon publish 29 new titles every month. Select from...

Modern Romance™   Tender Romance™

Sensual Romance™

Medical Romance™ Historical Romance™

MAT2